"Do I pass muster as an accomplice in crime, Mr. Dalton?" I asked saucily, to detain him a moment.

"No. I have just remembered another dereliction on my part. I left the kitchen lamp in Grindley's bedchamber. He will know, if he has his wits about him, that he had company."

"He will blame the servants."

"That chamber did not look to me as if it ever saw a servant from tip to toe of the week."

"True. It is difficult to comprehend a gentleman living in such a slovenly manner."

"Oh, we men are all savages beneath the skin. Prick any one of us, and you will find the primitive lurking."

"I do not think the savage is that close to the surface in you, Mr. Dalton."

"Don't count on it," he replied, with a suggestive smile. His tone, soft and low, spoke of romance. His hands rose and came slowly toward me, while his eyes glowed with admiration. His warm fingers touched my throat. The breath caught in my lungs, and just as I was about to close my eyes for a kiss, he removed the pearls from my neck.

THICK AS THIEVES

Jennie Gallant

FAWCETT CREST • NEW YORK

A Fawcett Crest Book
Published by Ballantine Books

Library of Congress Catalog Card Number: 92-97056

ISBN 0-449-22017-6

Manufactured in the United States of America

First Edition: January 1993

Chapter One

"BOTHER!" I DECLARED, glancing at the calendar. "Is it the end of May already? The butcher's bill is due, and my pockets are to let."

Aunt Hennie looked at me in alarm. She knew I had recently inherited thirty thousand pounds. Prior to this tremendous piece of luck, both sides of my family were mired in genteel poverty. It was Papa's second wife who brought him a fortune, and obligingly died before him. Lorene was a mean old bint, and I am not hypocrite enough to shed crocodile tears for her passing. I was truly shaken when Papa died a year later. I still miss him. Of course, I miss him a little less every day. It is ironic that Lorene's entire fortune came to me, whom she thoroughly disliked. I spent a year in Cornwall mourning Papa's death, then sold the house and traveled to London to place myself on the Marriage Mart. That was a year ago now, and I am still *Miss* Denver.

I had no idea it would prove so difficult to purchase a husband. It seems that in order to meet gents of the first stare, one must first make her debut at Court. In order to be presented to Queen Charlotte, one must have the proper connections. We made very few social connections in Cornwall. The fact that I am five and twenty is another obstacle. The mamas are yanking their daughters out of the schoolroom at a younger age every year.

While I rooted through my purse, Aunt Hennie

looked at the opulence surrounding us. My saloon was crowded with expensive cast-off furnishings of nobles who were obliged to hawk them to pay the grocer. Indeed, a satinwood commode had been added to the superfluity only that week. It cost me fifty pounds, and is worth a hundred easily. I snap up any such bargain I see, with the plan of removing to a larger mansion next year. On the walls there gleamed gilt frames holding paintings, not all of them good, but all done by fasionable and expensive artists. The Persian carpet beneath our feet had the honor of being trod on by a duchess last season.

"Must you pay the butcher today?" Hennie asked.

"I pay the merchants every six months, whether they dun me or no. I certainly must pay the butcher. He told Cook he is being married next week, and asked for his money."

"Perhaps I could lend you . . ."

I smiled indulgently. I knew to a penny that my aunt had a miserable two thousand pounds, which gave her roughly two pounds a week pocket money. How did she manage to look respectable on that pittance? I want to augment Auntie's fortune one of these days. She adamantly refuses to accept a salary for acting as my companion, saying that rack and manger are more than enough. I know she enjoys living in London—who would not, after the confinement of a small vicarage in Cranbrook? Auntie's late husband was vicar of St. Martin's.

"Not necessary, Auntie," I said. "It is a temporary shortage. I shall hawk a piece of jewelry." I swallowed a smile to see her goggle at this strategy. What a mousy little thing she was, all squinty gray eyes, gray gown, gray hair. Sometimes I forget she is even in the room.

"Could you return the satinwood commode?" she asked doubtfully.

I laughed merrily. "I could not part with Lord

Hutching's commode. I got it at a terrific bargain from a used-goods dealer in Shepherd's Market. I spotted a pawnshop right next door. We shall go there and place a piece of jewelry I never wear on the counter. Lorene used to take jewelry as collateral for loans. Half the time she got stuck with it. I shall use Mrs. Minton's ring. It has a good-sized diamond, but with a chip out of the corner."

I went up to my room to get the ring out of the safe and get my bonnet. I spared a peek at myself in the hall mirror before entering the saloon. No wonder Auntie found it hard to believe the fashionable dame staring back at me was short of money. I looked the picture of wealth, in my dashing feathered bonnet and teal blue walking suit with a fichu of Mechlin lace. Diamonds sparkled on both hands. The temporary financial shortfall did not hamper my spirits either.

I had been calling myself twenty-one for four years, and meant to continue this ruse until I found a husband. My dark hair, worn in a loose, fashionable coil, was touched with copper from the sunlight entering at the window. My green eyes were not so brilliant as emeralds, but the comparison was not laughable. My figure was good. I was always the energetic sort who preferred walking to driving, and riding to walking or any other mode of transportation. One thing that displeased me about London was the poor, shambling rides available at Rotten Row. If I do not marry a gentleman who has a country estate soon, I shall buy a little country property close to London, just for the pleasure of riding.

"I don't know what your papa would say if he knew we were going to a pawnshop," Auntie said with a daring smile when we were cutting through the London traffic in my dashing tilbury.

"A good thing he does not know," I replied airily. "Do not judge me by *your* high standards, Auntie.

I pay my bills, and do no harm to any man. We live differently in London, but we are not the dissipated creatures you think us. Where is the harm in borrowing money when you know you can pay it back?"

"I did not mean to criticize, dear," Hennie said hastily. "I know you are good. You handed that beggar a whole guinea the other day on Bond Street, and you are generous with your servants, to make up for your sharp tongue. Charity covers a multitude of sins."

Hennie's compliments usually come with a sharp edge. "Perhaps it is my self-indulgent life that appalls you? Theaters and drives . . ."

"Oh no! I never had such a wonderful time in my life. I shall never forget it."

A smug smile seized my face. I had done pretty well for a provincial solicitor's daughter. That was Papa's occupation when he met and married Lorene Hansom. She and Papa happened to be in London on business at the same time. They met at their hotel, and before you could say Jack Robinson, they were married. She had inherited mines and things from her papa. I could not abide Cornwall after Papa died. I lived there only seven years, but they were the years from eighteen to twenty-four, when I should have been meeting potential husbands. In Cornwall I never met a man I would want to spend an afternoon with, let alone a lifetime.

All that stifling tedium was over now. I was in London; I owned the elegant mansion I occupied on South Audley Street, and a small apartment house in town as well. Foster, my man of business, suggested I buy it with a small down payment and let my tenants pay off the mortgage.

The carriage drove south on South Audley to Curzon Street, turned south again, and we were suddenly in Shepherd's Market. It was a mean, narrow lane lined with mean establishments. The few men loitering about were not the sort ladies wished to encounter. A mangy yellow cur was hunched at one doorway, looking about with a hungry eye. I pulled the check string and asked the groom to have the owner come out to me. When in doubt, I take it as a rule of thumb that the ladylike thing to do is whatever is most comfortable for myself.

A moment later his head peered through the window. "Oi, the name's Parker," he said, offering a not very clean hand. He was a full-faced commoner with dark hair and beady eyes, the sort of man Papa would have called an oiler.

"I want to leave this ring in your safekeeping for a few days," I said. "I shan't take less than a hundred and fifty pounds, mind. It is worth a dozen times that. The stone is ten carats if it is anything."

Parker removed his head and the ring into the sunlight, stuck a loupe in his eye, and examined the stone. I noticed his finger touching the little chipped corner. Very likely he would use that as an excuse to bring down the price. His head reappeared and he said, "I can let you have fifty for it."

I reached out my hand. "Not interested, thank you. There are plenty of *reasonable* dealers about."

"We'll split the difference, missus. Seventy-five," he said, still holding on to the ring.

I wiggled my fingers imperiously. "Return my property, if you please. I could not possibly accept less than a hundred."

"A hundred it is then," Parker said, muttering for my benefit that he was a fool.

"I shall retrieve it in a week. Mind you don't sell it."

Parker drew the agreement up, right there in the street. He shoved a piece of paper into my hand, drew a roll of bills from his pocket, and counted out a hundred greasy pounds. I gave him the ring, and we were off.

"You always want to ask for fifty percent more than you will take," I explained to Hennie. "I could have got one twenty-five out of that fellow, if I had held out a bit longer." I glanced at the chit he had given me, and snorted. "Fifty percent interest per annum on the loan! Highway robbery! Let it be a lesson to me. Now, Hennie, where to? A scoot through Hyde Park to see the smarts and swells? Or shall we go to Bond Street for a bit of shopping?"

"Let us go to the park," she said. She was afraid the hundred pounds would never reach South Audley Street if I was let loose in a shop with the money. I *do* shop more than is necessary. At first, I needed a good many fashionable items. Now it has become a habit. When a lady has such a small circle of friends, shopping is one of the few genteel pastimes available to her. On that afternoon, however, we just drove to Hyde Park, and watched the ton disporting themselves.

It was always an agony to me, yet I kept at it. I felt very much an outsider when I saw the handsome young people talking and laughing together. They seemed to form a charmed circle, and I was the perpetual outsider. The few times I seemed about to crack society, I learned that my beau was a gazetted fortune hunter. One man I met at the theater, the other here at Hyde Park. I was not so eager to join the golden circle that I was willing to pay for it with Lorene's fortune.

I was not the sort of lady who had to wait until quarter day to receive my allowance. I had money invested in half a dozen different ventures. Interest checks and rent checks arrived at odd times of the year and month. It happened that some bonds Foster talked me into came due two days later.

"Let us go and retrieve the ring," I said to Hennie, and we were off to Shepherd's Market again.

Over the duration of her visit to London, Hennie's scruples were beginning to lose their razor edge. She was curious to see the inside of a pawnshop, and as neither dangerous loiterers nor dog impeded the visit, she allowed herself to be talked into going inside.

"You never know what treasure you might find at a good price," I explained. "A little out-of-the-way shop like this, hidden in the middle of a good neighborhood, might have some interesting jewelry. I should like to pick up an amethyst brooch to go with my new violet gown." I turned to the groom. "Walk the nags up to Curzon Street, Topby, and be back in ten minutes. We plan to have a look at the wares inside."

We went into the shop, and were immediately plunged into a foul-smelling darkness. The narrow window at front illuminated the first few yards of the shop, but the counter, farther back, was dim. I recognized Mr. Parker, however, and he recognized me. He was haggling with a customer who had a pile of trinkets displayed on the counter. In the dim light, it was impossible to assess either the worth of the objects or the appearance of the man. He had the well-modulated voice and good accent of a gentleman, but I was not interested in a gentleman sunk to selling the family jewels. He was selling, not pawning. A price was struck; the man took his money and left. As he walked toward the brighter front of the shop, I saw that he was blond, young, and rather handsome.

When I directed my attention back to Parker, he handed me Mrs. Minton's ring. I first thought it was the dim light that made it look so dull. Then I ran my finger over the edges, and felt a smoothness all around. "This is not my diamond!" I said.

He looked at the little tag he had attached to it.

"Surely it is, madam. You are Miss Denver, ain't you?"

Hennie paid us little heed. It was only to be expected that some altercation would arise. Aunt Hennie insists I enjoy a good argument. It is a rare day when even so simple a purchase as a bonnet or an ell of muslin could be completed without coming to cuffs with the clerk, but I maintain it is not my fault. In London, everyone and his dog are out to gyp you. You have to stand up for your rights or you will be palmed off with inferior seats at the theater, inferior food in restaurants, and inferior service wherever you go—all at ridiculously inflated prices.

"I tell you this is not the ring I left with you," I repeated, my voice rising.

"Be reasonable, Miss Denver," Parker said patiently. "It is exactly the same ring. Try it on; you'll see."

"Nonsense. You have pried out the diamond and stuck in a piece of glass. You don't catch me with an old stunt like that. I'll have my diamond, or I'll have the constable down on you."

"Are you threatening me?" Parker growled. His face had turned ugly.

"Yes, sir, I am!" From the corner of my eye, I noticed the pile of jewelry left on the counter by the other client. An emerald ring had become separated from the rest, sitting near me. It was edged in diamonds down either side. I was taken with it and thought I might buy it, if Parker were not such a crook.

He turned aside. "Get her, Duke," he said in a low voice. A black dog as big as a sideboard rose up from the floor. He wiped his slavering lips with a long tongue and made a lunge at me. Parker still held the leash. "Better get out while you can," he said, with an evil grin.

I don't know where the idea came from, for I am

really not a thief. I think it was Parker's sly, triumphant grin that goaded me to indiscretion. Without quite knowing what I was doing, my fingers closed over the emerald ring. "You have not heard the last of this, sir. I'll be back with a constable."

Parker released the dog, and Hennie and I darted to the door. A whistle called the dog back to his master.

I was trembling like a blancmange when we reached the street, and safety. "The crook!" I squealed.

"Eve, are you sure he stole your diamond?" Hennie asked.

"Of course he did, but he did not get the better of me!"

"What do you mean?"

I held out my hand and opened it, displaying the emerald ring. "You *stole* it!" Hennie gasped.

"I did not! I exchanged it for the diamond he pried out of my ring."

"But the poor man who hawked it—he will want it back."

"The fellow was selling it. I overheard the whole thing. Parker gave him a hundred pounds for it, the same as he allowed me on my diamond. They are of equivalent value, obviously."

"Oh my goodness. I feel weak." A vicar's widow, reared up in the countryside, had never before encountered this rough sort of justice.

Before she could succumb to a swoon, there was an awful bellowing behind us as Parker discovered my stunt and was after us, holding the black hound of hell on a rope. "Where is Topby?" I exclaimed.

"You told him to drive to Curzon Street. This way, run!" We took to our heels as fast as our legs could carry us.

"Stop them!" Parker hollered.

Looking ahead, I saw a constable fast approaching from Curzon Street, directly in our path. I grabbed Auntie's hand and pelted across the street. In my haste, I bumped into a man who was just about to ascend his carriage.

"Sorry," I gasped.

A blue arm came out to steady me. I glanced up, and saw a harsh face staring down at me. The face was lean and tanned. A pair of gray-green eyes, the very color of the Atlantic on a stormy day, looked startled.

"Are you all right?" he asked.

I looked over my shoulder, where Parker was gaining on us. From the other end of the lane, the constable was coming. He would find the emerald on me and arrest me. Visions of the Old Bailey and Bridewell flashed through my mind. I used Hennie's advance to nudge up closer to the gentleman. "Don't let us detain you," I said, taking Hennie's arm to hasten her along. My other hand hovered over the man's pocket, and I slid the emerald ring into it, brushing against him to conceal the movement of my hand.

"Where to, Mr. Dalton?" the man's groom called from his perch.

"Hyde Park," Dalton replied.

I saw him glance at the approaching constable, and wondered at his lack of curiosity in leaving at this exciting juncture. If it were me, I would have waited to see what was going forth. In fact, I was struck with the notion that Mr. Dalton was in a hurry to escape himself. Perhaps he just did not want to be involved as a witness in some unsavory case. "Are you sure you're all right?" he asked.

"We're fine, thank you," I assured him.

He climbed into his coach and it rattled off. I was glad the nice man got away before I was utterly disgraced, but I still thought it odd.

The constable and Parker reached us at the same time. "Arrest her. She's robbed me of an emerald ring," Parker said.

"There is your thief!" I retaliated, pointing at Parker.

A loud and excessively vulgar wrangle ensued. We went into Parker's shop to escape the gawking crowd. Hennie and I endured the indignity of having our reticules and pockets searched. I gradually got the idea that the constable had some familiarity with Parker's unsavory reputation. His attitude seemed to be that if someone had got the better of him, so much the better.

"We'll leave it up to the courts," he said. "You, madam, can bring a charge against Parker. And you, Parker, can do likewise, if you want to be bitten to death by lawyers. It is up to you. Do you want to lay charges, folks?"

Parker and I exchanged an angry, knowing look. "It is not worth my while," I said grandly, "but I shall warn my friends to avoid this establishment."

"I can do without *your* friends, thankee. Maybe the ring fell on the floor. I'll have a look," Parker said, and began to make a show of looking around the floor.

Hennie and I ducked out to the waiting carriage. "Where to, madam?" Topby called.

"Hyde Park," I replied.

Chapter Two

We took a moment to recover our breaths. "What did you do with the ring, Eve? I made sure they would find it in your pocket, and we would end up in Bridewell," Hennie said, when she could speak.

"I got rid of it when I saw the constable coming."

"You threw it away?"

"Certainly not. I slid it in that gentleman's pocket, the man I bumped into. He was handsome, was he not? That is why we are going to Hyde Park." Hennie smirked. She has the idea that I am interested in nothing but finding a husband. She is quite mistaken; I want a circle of female friends, too. I am tired of being an Ishmael. "To recover the ring, Hennie. He directed his groom to Hyde Park. Keep an eye out for him when we get there."

"I am sure you will spot him, Eve," she said snidely.

"His carriage was plain black. Not a coroneted door. I rather hoped he might be a lord."

Overcome by a belated seizure, Hennie dissolved into a fit of giggles. "You are up to all the rigs. You even noticed his carriage lacked a lozenge. I made sure you would go straight home and dose yourself with hartshorn, as I feel like doing."

"Why, there is no need to go home to do that. I have a bottle right here. What an excellent idea. I am feeling shaken myself." I drew a small cut-glass bottle from my reticule and unscrewed the lid to inhale the spirits of ammonia. When my eyes were watering and my lungs felt as if they were being pricked with pins, I gave Hennie the bottle to have a whiff.

"I wonder who he can be," she said. Her breaths were shallow from the ammonia.

"I have no idea. Unfortunately, we do not know his sort." I meant the sort who inhabited the charmed circle. "I hope he is still at the park, or we have lost our ring."

"How shall we approach him, if he is there?" she asked. "He must have seen the constable coming after us."

"Would he believe the truth, do you think, or should we invent some tale to appeal to his chivalry?"

"Much better to avoid the truth," she replied, sinking ever deeper into sin. Her late husband adhered to the credo that no motive was strong enough to excuse a lie. I knew this apropos my unchanging age over the years. Indeed, the phrase "mutton dressed as lamb" had been used on one occasion.

"You are right. He might take into his head to go calling the constable. I shall, hopefully, bump into him 'by accident' at the park, and tell him I lost my ring. I shall say I had it in my hand when I met him, and ask him if he would just mind having a look in his pocket, in case it fell in there. He can hardly refuse such a simple request."

"He'll have a look if he knows what is good for him," she said—another little dig at my temper.

A memory of his harsh face lingered at the back of my mind. He did not seem a man to be led by a shrew. The face's undeniable harshness had not been softened by the concern in his eyes. I remembered every feature of his face in peculiarly vivid detail. No doubt my perceptions had been heightened at the time due to the piquant circumstances. How else to account for the vivid memory of his crisp black hair, those strong black brows, that slightly hawkish nose? He had been tall; he towered a good six inches above me, and I am five and a half feet. Either his blue jacket had wadding, or his shoulders were very broad and straight. As his stomach was as flat as an ironing board, I gave him the benefit of the doubt.

"How can we explain about the constable?" Hennie said, interrupting my reveries.

"Dalton cannot know the man was after us. We shall say someone had a purse snatched."

She turned pious on me. "David always said—"

I rudely cut off her repetition of the late vicar's ideas about lying. "Yes, Hennie. I know what David always said. I hope Dalton descends from his carriage. Would you recognize it again? Plain black, with a pair of matched bays, was it not?"

"I did not notice the team," she replied vaguely.

I assumed she was warring with her conscience over the projected tissue of lies, and left her to it.

As we drove through Hyde Park, Hennie exclaimed, "There! That is him!" She pointed out the window to Mr. Dalton, who stood in conversation with a fashionable blond lady, dressed in the first style of elegance. I had seen, admired, and envied the lady before; she was a certified member of the ton. She was often seen on the strut on Bond Street, at the barrier at Hyde Park, on the grand tier at the theaters, and no doubt at fashionable parties from which I was excluded. What roused my curiosity was that I had not seen her with Mr. Dalton before.

"He is not alone," I said, disappointed. "The blonde could be his sweetheart. You do the talking, Hennie. His girlfriend will resent having another lady chasing after her beau."

"I would not know what to say!" Hennie exclaimed.

As she would certainly make a botch of it, I relented and agreed to do the lying myself. I pulled the check string and we descended. The clement weather made a walk unexceptionable. The sun shone brightly, fuzzing the greenery of grass and trees with a tinge of gold. Bird song filled the air, and a warm zephyr caressed our cheeks. The pathways were full of strolling fashionables as we wended our way toward Dalton.

When he espied us, he gave a sudden start of recognition, just before his eyes widened, revealing rampant curiosity. He recognized us, certainly. I only hoped he had not discovered the ring, and begun suspecting our integrity. Our eyes met, and I drew to a stop. "It is you!" I exclaimed, as if in surprise.

"I am happy to see you escaped from your—difficulties," he said, hesitating over what to call our former predicament.

"Yes, I understand some poor lady had her purse snatched, and the constable was running after the fellow."

"Did they catch him?"

"We did not linger in such a horrid location," I said demurely, and immediately turned to smile at the lady, to divert his conversation and her wrath at my knowing Dalton while not knowing her.

"Allow me to present my sister, Lady Filmore," he said. "Linda, this is—I do not have your names, ladies." He smiled.

I introduced first myself, then Hennie. You may be sure I took careful note that his companion was his sister. She had all the accoutrements of an Incomparable—blond curls, blue eyes, rose petal skin, teeth of pearl, French gown, etc.

Lady Filmore told us that her brother—she called him Richard—had mentioned the little fracas in Shepherd's Market, and chided us for going to such a verminous place. We stayed chatting a moment, working around to asking for the ring. Lady Filmore was an inestimable help. She was a regular chatterbox.

Over the next few moments, we learned that Lady Filmore (Linda) was not only married but widowed, at nineteen years of age. I wondered if her husband had left her unprovided for, since she made her home with Mr. Dalton. Soon it came out that she already had another beau in her eye.

"Let us sit and rest our legs," she suggested. "I want to talk about Brighton, Richard. Let us go there this week. The Season ends tomorrow. Everyone will be running off to Brighton. You have that handsome house on Marine Parade, sitting idle."

"Lord Harelson, I assume, will be going to Brighton?" he replied with a quizzing smile that spoke of romance.

"He mentioned going today," she laughed.

Much as I enjoyed having someone other than Hennie to talk with in the park, I sensed we had outstayed our welcome. "We will leave you to it, Lady Filmore," I said. "We must be running along now, but before we go—foolish me!" I turned a fluttering gaze on Dalton. "I was carrying an emerald ring I had just redeemed from the pawnbroker when I bumped into you at Shepherd's Market, Mr. Dalton. I know I had it in my hand when I bumped into you, and a moment later, it was gone. We went back and scoured the street with a fine-tooth comb. It is extremely unlikely, I know, but do you think it might just possibly have fallen into your pocket?" We walked on a little way.

Dalton slid his hand into his pocket, and brought it out empty. "It seems not," he said.

His expression was perfectly bland, yet I was morally certain the man was lying. So much for the ton! "Try the other pocket. It must be there," I said. He tried the other pocket, with the same result. "Would you happen to have a hole in your pocket?"

I asked, my voice becoming thin with annoyance. He turned his pockets out, so that I could see they were empty, but in good repair. I could only stare in disbelief. It was impossible! I soon concluded that he had found the ring, and was concealing it from me. Stealing it, in other words.

"You must be mistaken, Eve," Auntie said.

"Mistaken, is it?" I asked, eyes fulminating.

"Perhaps it fell out into my carriage," Dalton suggested. He certainly knew the way my mind was veering. I should not have been a bit surprised if he also suspected I had hidden the ring to avoid detection.

"Where is your carriage?" I demanded.

"Unfortunately I had it taken to the stable when I called on my sister. She wished to take her own carriage. I shall have mine searched and take the ring to you if it is found, if you will give me your address, Miss Denver."

I told him, but I had very little hope of ever seeing the ring again, and wished to learn where this new thief resided.

"We are practically neighbors, ma'am. I live on Grosvenor Square," he said, without my even asking.

"Then you will not have to go far out of your way to return the ring. I am sure you will find it in your carriage. Where else could it be?" I added, in a rhetorical spirit.

"Where else indeed? Will you be home this evening?"

"You may be very sure of it, sir. If it is not in your carriage, I must take other steps," I said, flashing a menacing glance at him. Of course, it was hopeless. Who was to say he even lived in Grosvenor Square?

"Yes indeed. You will want to speak to Bow Street," he replied, unfazed. "Good afternoon, Miss Denver." He turned to Hennie. "And Mrs. Henderson." Did I imagine a lurking ray of mischief in that cold gray eye?

His sister got tired of waiting and arose from the bench. She beckoned Dalton to her, waved to us, and we left.

"She is not his wife," Hennie said, smiling.

"If I had not seen her in Lady Jersey's carriage last week, I would think she was his lightskirt, and he a common thief. He *must* have found that ring in his pocket. It could not have jumped out and run away by itself."

"You think Mr. Dalton stole it from you?"

"Of course he did. We'll not see him at South Audley Street if I know anything. I'll be demmed if I know what to do next, Hennie. I fear we have been bested in this affair."

"David always said it is hard for a rich man to get into heaven. Something about a camel and the eye of a needle."

"The ton are no better than they should be. We shall go home and have a glass of wine to settle our nerves." We went to the carriage and were driven home.

"I think he will come," Hennie said. She is not really a simpleton, but her lack of experience sometimes makes her appear one. I snorted my disagreement.

Chapter Three

"YOU HAD BEST run up and tidy your hair, Hennie," I suggested that evening after dinner. "We leave for the theater in five minutes." I had ceased my oft-dropped hint that she stick a plume in her coiffure for fashion's sake. I knew what she would say. "If the Lord wanted me to wear feathers, he would have given me wings."

"Leave!" she exclaimed in dismay. "You forget Mr. Dalton is to call this evening, Eve."

I had made an especially fine toilette in his honor, (bronze crepe with gold ribbons), but it was not in my saloon I expected to see him. A new play was opening at Drury Lane. I had often seen Lady Filmore there. As Lord Harelson had removed to Brighton, I thought she might make Dalton take her.

My chestnut hair was scooped up in dainty curls in an effort to remove half a decade from my five and twenty years. Mr. Dalton looked about thirty. I have often noticed that the older a gentleman is, the younger his lady friends. It is only younger gentlemen who are impressed by "older" ladies.

I said to Hennie, "I doubt he will come. And if he does, what is to prevent him from leaving the ring with the butler? I shall ask Tumble to be on the lookout for him."

"You told him we would be here," she pointed out.

"Good gracious, he would not expect us to sit

home all evening waiting for him. You may be sure a swell like Dalton is on the town himself. He would have dropped it off before going out to dinner, if he had any intention of returning it."

"I daresay you are right," she said, with a sad look. "Unfortunately, your poor view of people has frequently proven right in the past. But if he does bring the ring while we are out, we must call on him and thank him properly."

"I will be only too happy to do it."

As the words left my mouth, the front door knocker sounded. We exchanged a surprised look. Soon Dalton's baritone voice was heard asking for us. I had scarcely time to arrange my bronze skirt artfully about me before Tumble showed him in.

Dalton made his bows. I noticed his sharp eyes glancing off the prismatic sparkle of genuine diamonds at my throat, and around the room at the handsome array of old furnishings I had collected. If he was assessing my worth, I concluded he had also taken an inventory of the house from outside. It is smallish, but in an excellent neighborhood. He must realize there was money here from somewhere.

He turned his bow to Auntie. Before he said a word, Hennie spoke. "Did you find the ring?" she asked with eager vulgarity.

"I am happy to tell you I did," he replied. He withdrew it from his pocket and handed it to me.

"Well, upon my word!" I exclaimed. "I never thought to see this beauty again." My joy was doubled in that Mr. Dalton was proven an honest man.

"I trust that is not a slur on my honesty, ma'am," he said playfully.

"Certainly not. It is merely a comment on my luck. Thank you for bringing the ring. Have you time for a glass of wine?"

"I judge by your elegant toilettes that you ladies

are going out," he replied, using it as an excuse to ogle me. "You must not let me detain you."

"No hurry, sir. One does not arrive on time for a rout, or folks think you have been sitting, waiting for it to begin."

"A rout?" Hennie said, in a questioning tone.

I stared her down and rang for Tumble, who came and poured the wine. Tumble had done service in the stately homes of England, and had been hired for his appearance and his social skills. He looks as a butler should look, which is to say like a gentleman without any sense of humor whatsoever. When he is sober, he is an excellent butler. I trusted his instincts would prevent him from mentioning that my carriage was waiting, and that if I did not hop it, I would be late for the play.

Dalton accepted the wine and sat down for a little chat. "I hope you will not think it presumptuous of me, Miss Denver," he said, "but I am very curious to hear why you took your ring to Parker." His eyes slid around the room, finding enough valuable furniture and artwork there to furnish two saloons. "That fellow is not quite the thing, you must know."

"He is as crooked as a dog's hind leg," I said with some warmth. "I know perfectly well he pried the diamond out of a ring I left with him, and replaced it with glass."

"Ah, you pawned two rings," he said, nodding wisely.

"Just the one, actually," Hennie said.

Dalton frowned in forgivable confusion. "I must have misunderstood. You said this afternoon that you had just redeemed this emerald ring."

"Redeemed is *one* way of putting it," Hennie said.

Dalton looked so suspicious that I decided to enlighten him before he thought me worse than I was. I did not feel my action was stealing, in the normal sense of the word.

In short, I confessed the whole seamy business,

holding back only that I had purposely put the emerald ring in his pocket. He did not call me a thief, but I sensed an air of disapproval about him. The Atlantic eyes turned darker and stormier as I spoke. "Strange he should have a paste stone of the proper size to replace your diamond," he said.

"He had a couple of days to acquire one, Mr. Dalton. Here, this is the ring he removed the diamond from," I said, drawing it from my reticule, where I had tossed it that afternoon. "Glass, you see. It was a diamond when I left it there two days before." I explained about the small chip in one corner.

Dalton examined it carefully. "I can see the tool marks on the mounting prongs," he said. "This was obviously a rushed job." Then he lifted his head and smiled. "Allow me to congratulate you on your swift thinking, Miss Denver."

"She really ought not to have done it," Hennie said uncertainly. Her lingering sense of morality expected some condemnation from Mr. Dalton.

"Mrs. Henderson's late husband was a vicar," I explained.

"At St. Martin's, in Cranbrook," Hennie added.

"A fine old perpendicular church, if memory serves?"

"Yes, have you seen it?" she asked, brightening.

"Only from the outside."

"You should tour it next time you are in Cranbrook, Mr. Dalton. It has an old baptistry for complete immersion, dating from the eighteenth century. We did not use it, of course."

"I seem to remember hearing something of the sort."

I had the peculiar feeling that Hennie's being a vicar's widow raised us in Dalton's esteem. It is hard to describe, but a new sort of warmth entered his conversation. It was as if he had not quite believed my story, but Hennie's clerical association removed the doubt.

There followed some general conversation peppered throughout by a series of discreet questions that eventually revealed our harmless history. Of course, I did not crop out into an announcement of my fortune, but my circumstances hinted at one. The dread question as to why I had not made my bows arose, to be shuffled aside by a mendacious mention of my lack of interest in society. While we talked, his eyes darted from time to time to the emerald ring, resting on the sofa table.

"That emerald ring looks familiar," he said, frowning as if trying to remember. "Now, where have I seen it before?" Hennie handed it to him, to aid his memory. "Ah! I have it now! It belonged to Lady Dormere."

Hennie nodded. "That satinwood commode belonged to Lord Hutching. Eve bought it from the antique shop next door to Parker's place. That is how she came to know about Parker."

"Really?" He glanced at the commode, and at a dark old portrait above it, purchased at the same time for its nice gilt frame. Then he looked back at the ring. "I seem to remember some story about this ring," he said, frowning again. "I think—yes, by God, I have it now. This was stolen by Tom, the famous burglar who is lifting all the ladies' jewels."

"You never mean it!" I gasped. Although the name Tom has not occurred formerly in this tale, it was a name frequently read in the journals that year. England was rife with thieves. A highwayman by the name of Black Bart was also on the prowl.

It was for the vicar's widow to suggest doing the right thing. "You must give it back to her, Eve," she exclaimed.

"And who will give me back my diamond, that Parker pried out of my ring?" I demanded.

"That is not Lady Dormere's fault," she pointed out.

"It is not my fault either," I said sharply. "I don't know what the world is coming to. People snatching what does not belong to them. Tom, the burglar, has been terrorizing society for over a year now, and never a move to stop him."

"You are mistaken there, Miss Denver," Dalton said. "I have been Tom's victim, but I *am* doing something to try to stop him. In fact, that was why I was loitering outside of Parker's place this afternoon. A friend of mine bought a brooch from Parker, then learned it was part of Tom's loot. I have been keeping a watch on the place. If the same fellow went in frequently, then it would suggest he was trafficking in stolen goods. Perhaps you wondered at my sudden departure, just when events had reached such an interesting pitch," he said, smiling. "I did not wish Parker to see me."

"Have you had any luck in catching Tom?" Hennie asked him.

"No, I followed up on one or two fellows who were selling stolen goods to Parker, but they were associated with Stop Hole Abbey. I fancy Tom sells his goods at more than one place."

"What is Stop Hole Abbey?" she asked.

"It is a sort of clearing ground for stolen goods. The thieves take their wares there. They are sold for a small fraction of their value to fences, who frequently break the jewelry up and sell the stones. We have not traced Tom to Stop Hole Abbey, however. He works strictly alone. When his goods appear, they are still in one piece, like this emerald ring, and the diamond brooch my friend bought."

"The best way to catch a mouse is to set a trap," I said. "Why wait at the hole, when you suspect Tom has more than one hole? Bait some rich lady's house with diamonds, set the word about that she has gone on holiday, and he will soon show up."

"But where to find this obliging lady?" Dalton asked. "And now, of course, the Season is over. Tom will remove his business to Brighton, where he began his illustrious career last summer. I shall be going there myself."

I tried to hide my disappointment. "When will you leave, Mr. Dalton?" I inquired, with no more than civil interest.

"Tomorrow. I have to take my leave of a few people this evening. I really should be getting on with it," he said. Yet he seemed in no hurry to stand up and go. Indeed, unless I am imagining things, there was a sad smile in his eyes at the thought of leaving. Here was the very sort of parti I hoped to find. With my usual luck, he was slipping away the very day I met him. One of Hennie's oft-repeated sayings came to me, viz, "The Lord helps those who help themselves." What was to prevent me from going to Brighton? It was only a lack of imagination that held me in London, when all the ton would be leaving.

"We have been speaking of removing to Brighton ourselves," I said. My eyes flew to Hennie's open mouth, warning her to silence. She closed her mouth, then opened it and closed it a few more times, like a fish out of water.

"Have you been in touch with an estate agent?" he asked.

"No, not yet."

"I fear you will find houses in short supply, having left it so late. What sort of house did you have in mind?"

"Nothing too large, just a pied-à-terre for two," I said.

He nodded and said, "I happen to know of a nice house that is standing empty. It is near the ocean, not too large, but not a tumbledown cottage either." I emitted sounds of interest, and Hennie sat, struck dumb, thank God. He continued. "The reason I happen to know of the place is that it belongs to my neighbor, Lady Grieve. She will not be using it this season, but unfortunately she does not rent it."

My surging hopes plunged. Why did he bother telling us of it if it was not for hire? "Foolish of her," I scoffed. "What harm would a couple of mature ladies like Mrs. Henderson and myself do to it? It is not as though we would be holding wild parties, nor bring a houseful of kiddies to write on the walls and soil the carpets."

"That is true," Dalton said. "I could mention it to Lady Grieve, if you like. We have been neighbors there for years, and are good friends. She might do it to please me."

"That would be most obliging of you," I said.

Before he left, it was agreed that he would call on Lady Grieve that same night, and let us know before he left in the morning. In fact, he drove directly to Lady Grieve from South Audley Street, and was back inside half an hour with the good news. Lady Grieve's only stipulation was that I must hire her gardener to keep an eye on the grounds. I quickly acceded to that, as I had no gardener, and thought one servant familiar with the house and the town would be to our advantage.

"I expect you will want to see the house before signing the contract," he said. "I suggest you drive to Brighton with me tomorrow to look it over. If you approve, we shall return and sign the contract."

"That is too much trouble for you, Mr. Dalton," I objected at once, although I appreciated the offer. "If you say the house is in good repair, then I shall take your word for it."

"When will you come?" he inquired with obvious eagerness.

"We shall arrive the day after tomorrow. One or two servants can go down in advance to prepare for our arrival while I take care of my business here."

"You must dine with Lady Filmore and me the

first evening," he said. "We shall invite a few friends to meet you. Linda will be happy to show you around town the next day."

"That is very kind of you both," I said to Dalton.

"I would be happy to spare you another nuisance, if you like. I shall be taking my leave of Lady Dormere in the morning. Shall I return her ring, and save you the bother?"

My incipient scowl withered to a smile, when I considered Dalton's many kindnesses that evening. "Thank you," I said, and took the ring from the table to give him.

"I trust you have taken precautions against Tom for the safety of your other jewelry, Miss Denver?" he asked.

"Yes indeed. I have a safe right in my bedroom." He nodded his approval, we said good night, and he left.

I went to bed that night with my head in a whirl. In one fell stroke I had cut a path into the charmed circle of the ton. Soon I would be dining with Lady Filmore and Dalton, and I would be hard put to say whether the host or hostess thrilled me more. They were inviting friends to meet me. The unfortunate affair of the stolen diamond had turned out well after all. Hennie had no holy aphorism to offer that evening.

After an hour's gloating, less pleasant thoughts wafted into my head. What if Dalton did not return the ring to Lady Dormere? I had only his word for it that it belonged to her. Indeed, I had only his word for any of my bright future; that the mysterious Lady Grieve existed, and was willing to rent me her house. But then, he had returned the ring voluntarily. If he meant to steal it, why bother to return it at all?

There is nothing so enervating as a sleepless night. I heard the church bells ring three o'clock. By that time, I was more than half-convinced I was a fool, and Dalton a scoundrel. I consoled myself that all I had really lost was the chipped diamond from Mrs. Minton's ring, and the price of the unused tickets for Drury Lane that evening. With that consolation, I finally slept.

Chapter Four

I WOKE EARLY enough the next morning to witness the miracle of sunrise. That wise old alchemist, Sun, changed the leaden skies to fiery gold before my very eyes. I watched, enchanted, as gray faded to pearly white, tinged with pale saffron, then the rim of fire appeared, gilding the heavens. My nightmares had left me, as you may have guessed by that poetic outburst. One ought not to think too much in bed at night. In daylight, I decided that Mr. Dalton was a gentleman, and everything was going to be fine.

When I joined Hennie at the breakfast table, a hand-delivered letter bearing a crest awaited me. I snatched it up eagerly. "It is from Lady Dormere!" I exclaimed. "She thanks me for returning her emerald, and says she will call on me when I return from Brighton. Is that not marvelous, Hennie?"

"It is the least she can do. I thought she might be offering a reward. In Cranbrook when Mrs. Forrester lost her watch, she gave Billie Seymore a half crown for finding it."

"We cannot expect Lady Dormere to achieve such heights of perfection as a doctor's wife."

My real joy was less for Lady Dormere's condescension than for this tangible proof that Mr. Dalton had returned the ring. Even my suspicious nature could not imagine that he had had time to get stationery bearing the lady's crest made up, and forged a note. Hennie was glancing at the newspaper while I reread the note.

"Listen to this, Eve!" she said. "Here it is, right in black and white, that we are going to Brighton."

"Impossible! We have not told a soul except Mr. Dalton."

"See for yourself." She passed the journal over, and I read that the many friends of Miss Denver, the Cornwall tin heiress, and her companion, Mrs. Henderson, would be interested to hear that the ladies had taken Lady Grieve's lovely mansion on Marine Parade in Brighton for the summer.

"How on earth did the papers get hold of this?" I asked. Actually, I was as pleased as punch. "The many friends," while ludicrious, had a lovely sound to it. I had no objection to the "Cornwall tin heiress" either. This would make the ton sit up and take notice. I ought to have inserted such an advertisement when I first came to London.

When Mr. Dalton came in person at ten o'clock, I could scarcely believe I had ever mistrusted him. Who could mistrust a gentleman in such a well-cut jacket, smelling vaguely of some piney scent, and driving such a well-matched team of bays?

"I am just about to leave for Brighton," he said, but he agreed to sit down and have a cup of coffee with us.

I showed him Lady Dormere's note, and he told me how delighted she was to recover her ring. "I am afraid I was not entirely truthful," he said. The sun glinted in his Atlantic eyes that morning. "I told her only that you had got the ring from Parker. I did not go into details as to the nature of your procuring it. She assumed you bought it, believing it to have been left on the shelf by someone. I tell you this as she is eager to meet you, and thank you in person."

"What a shabby creature you must think me," I

said, smiling in that careless way I had often admired in the ton.

"On the contrary, I admire your daring."

Hennie shoved the journal under his nose. "Look at this, Mr. Dalton," she said. "Here is Eve's and my name in the journals, right alongside Lady Jersey's and the Princess Lieven's. We are flying pretty high these days."

"I cannot imagine how the press got hold of it," I said with a *tsk*, as though annoyed.

"Did you not wish it to be known?" he inquired, wearing a worried face. "I am afraid this is my fault. When my sister was sending off her notice last night, I happened to wonder aloud if you had remembered to do so. She felt you had probably not, as your decision was taken suddenly. She did it for you, to let your friends know where you were to be found."

"That is quite all right. Very kind of her," I said magnanimously. "It did slip my mind, actually. It is as well for my friends to know, or they might be wondering."

Hennie's lips twitched in either condemnation or amusement at my speech. After a cup of coffee, it was decided that Mr. Dalton would take our butler to Brighton in his rig, to prepare our house for us. I felt Tumble would give him a better impression of our household than any of the other servants. He was bound to be sober this early in the day. We parted on the best of terms, with a promise to meet for dinner in Brighton on the morrow.

The remainder of the day was a turmoil of activity. Although I had few friends, I had considerable business to attend to. It had to be thrashed out which servants were to remain on South Audley Street, as I did not wish to leave the house empty. Jimmie Polke, who had come with me from Cornwall, had family in Cheapside and was eager to stay in London. The others were eager for a whiff of sea air, so that was soon settled. I visited my solicitor and man of business to arrange for having my monies and bills sent to Brighton. In a merry mood, I stopped at the millinery shop and purchased not less than two bonnets, one a romantic leghorn with a wide brim that could not possibly be worn anywhere but at a garden party, but it looked very dashing. Lady Filmore wore one similar in her portrait at the recent exhibition at Somerset House.

Hennie made a dashing visit to her clergyman, to explain that we would not be occupying a pew in his church for a few months. "He will be missing your guinea in the collection plate, Eve," she said a few times, until I got the idea I was to put all my guineas in an envelope before leaving, and she would take them to him. We remained at home that evening, tending to the last-minute chores of toilette, and retired early. No dark thoughts troubled my sleep. My head no sooner hit the pillow than I was out like a lamp, to awaken in the morning fresh as a flower, eager to be off to Brighton.

I hoped to get away by ten, but with last-minute conferences with Polke, and with our groom suddenly remembering that we really ought to have four horses, which meant a trip to Newman's stable, we did not leave until eleven. It was rumored that our Prince Regent, in his heyday, made the trip from Brighton to London in his curricle in approximately four hours. I can only conclude that his speed, like so much about the man, is a sham. With my own team plus the hired pair, it took us over seven hours of hard rattling, and we made only one hasty stop to eat and refresh ourselves.

We arrived around six, and were immediately enchanted with the place. Brighton rests on the seaward slope of the South Downs. The oceanfront is on a shallow bay. Had I never been to London, I would have thought it a huge metropolis. Our carriage continued south right to the water. The sea was no stranger to me, after my sojourn at Cornwall, but here was a civilized sea, not the stormy rolls and barren rocky cliffs of the west coast. The waters are tamed by the Channel, I daresay. Only the smell was similar, a lingering tang of salt and seaweed and fish, the latter not overwhelming by any means, despite Hennie's asking for my hartshorn and applying it to her nose. I must buy her a bottle, as she seems perpetually in need of it.

Mr. Dalton's house was on Marine Parade, at the corner of Bedford Street. Lady Grieve's was right next door. Both were brick and of modern vintage, which is to say, built within the last thirty odd years, since Priney made Brighthelmston famous, increasing its size and shortening its name. My house (from henceforth Lady Grieve's house shall be termed my house) was not quite so large or fine as Mr. Dalton's mansion, but had a prettier garden at the back. I determined on the spot that I would have an alfresco party there some fine afternoon to show off my leghorn bonnet.

Tumble met us at the doorway (sober, but smelling of gin) and welcomed us into a dark-paneled hall. There was a deal too much dark paneling in the whole house to suit me, but other than that, it was entirely suitable, indeed a little grander than I had anticipated. Taking into account the excellent location, I felt we had struck a good bargain. The place was well got up with good old furniture but with a sad surfeit of bibelots and fading prints. I would remove the bibelots and replace the prints with some of my own pictures from London. And perhaps my silk Persian carpet, to replace the threadbare thing in the main saloon. Lady Grieve could not be so intransigent as to forbid these temporary improvements.

Tumble handed me a note from Lady Filmore, bidding us to dinner at seven-thirty. This was pretty late for Hennie. We usually kept country hours, even in London. We asked Tumble for tea to refresh us after our long drive, and while it was prepared, we chose our bedrooms. There were five in all, two nice large ones giving a view of the sea, and three smaller at the back of the house with a view of the garden. I hardly know which view was more enchanting, but I wanted a larger room, and so did Hennie. There was a third floor for the servants.

I was most eager to get out exploring the town, but with the treat of Lady Filmore's dinner party awaiting us, there was not time that evening. As soon as we had supped our tea, we went abovestairs to make our toilettes. With no grand parties to require the services of a professional dresser, Hennie and I were in the habit of helping each other, using Mary Day for the odd fancy do that came our way. (Mostly the theater. If one could not buy a ticket for a do, we were unlikely to be there.)

In her note, Lady Filmore used the phrase "an informal evening to meet a few friends." I was quite at a loss as to what this dasher would consider either "informal" or "a few." Hennie was of the simple-minded idea that "informal" meant informal, and "a few" meant three or four. I was glad I paid her no heed. As the hour drew near, I kept an eye on the window to watch the stream of carriages draw up at her door, and the toilettes of the ton descending from them.

At seven-twenty I changed my pearls for diamonds. At seven twenty-five, I took the brush to my curls and redid my simple coil to a more exotic thing, with loops over the ears. When a lady wearing chiffon and an ermine-tipped wrap descended from a crested carriage at seven-thirty, I made a hasty scramble out of my blue lutestring gown into my best outfit, doing considerable damage to the loops of hair in the process. At seven thirty-five I was ready, decked out in an "informal" gown of rose satin, wearing diamonds and the aforesaid exotic hairdo. My stomach was in knots, and my hands were shaking.

Five minutes later, Lady Filmore welcomed us into a gracious saloon done up in pale shades of green watered moire that gave the curious effect of being in the sea, rather than beside it. She was wearing a silk gown of French cut that might have been called informal by Marie Antoinette, perhaps. It was not overly ornate, but it reeked of elegance. Bits of blond lace showed at the top, and minute green bows littered the skirt. Her hair was fluffed about her ears in soft curls. Perhaps that was what she meant by informal. I felt my hair was hideously overdone. We brushed cheeks in a ritual kiss, and expressed the greatest delight in meeting again.

"You probably know everyone," she said, drawing us into the middle of a crowd of perfect strangers.

After the introductions, I could not recall a single name except Lord Harelson. He was a tall, slender, blond dandy, nearly as pretty as Lady Filmore. He wore an expression of weary disdain, and had petulant lips. I did catch an occasional "Lord" this or "Lady" that during the introductions, but what came after the title invariably sounded like a vegetable. Cauliflower, or broccoli, or some long string of uncertain syllables. I noticed in particular that there was not a sign of Mr. Dalton anywhere. This unnerved me to no small extent. I had thought I would have at least one friend in the house, if I may call a gentleman of two days' acquaintance a friend.

Lady Cauliflower (or perhaps it was Collifer, or Col something) drew a chair up beside mine and began to coze as if we were bosom bows. She was a gruff-voiced grenadier of a lady with white hair. "You have taken Grieve's place," she informed me. I could not deny it, though it sounded like an accusation. "A shocking dark old dungeon."

"But the gardens are pretty."

"Aye, they are. I daresay she conned you into paying her gardener for her?"

"The gardener is staying on."

"I thought as much. I hired the dungeon one season. That is what the locals call it. Never again. It is a pity that was the only house left unrented. It is always the last to go."

"I did not realize Lady Grieve was in the habit of hiring it," I said. You will realize why this struck me as noteworthy.

"She usually manages to get a taker at the last minute. There is a fortune to be made in Brighton if some sharp person with blunt put up a decent set of flats for hire, as they have done in Bath. It could be done for under fifty thousand. Now, there is something *you* could think of doing with your blunt, Miss Denver."

"What an interesting idea," I said, with whatever remained of my wits. Where had she walked away with the notion that I had that kind of money to spend? She had obviously read the notice in the London journals, and overestimated my worth.

Ere long she darted off to have a word with Hennie, and her seat was taken by Lord Broccoli, who turned out to be Lord Brockley. A natural error on my part. He was a stumpy little fellow, built unusually low to the ground, like a chimpanzee. What remained of his hair was a pretty chestnut color, growing in a circle around his head, with a bald spot showing on top. He used a quizzing glass and had snuff spilled down the front of his waistcoat. He was dressed all in gray, like Hennie.

"You would be our tin heiress," he said, spearing me with a sharp blue eye. "Hired the Grieve's dungeon. Pity. Read about it in the Brighton *Bugle*."

"Was it in the Brighton papers, too?"

"This morning. Causing a good bit of stir, m'dear. And your aunt as well. A fine-looking lady. Is she also from Cornwall?"

"From Cranbrook, actually." I had a feeling "from Cornwall" meant "did she also own a tin mine?"

"You want to keep a weather eye out for the fortune hunters. We get a deal of them here in the summer. Dalton will keep an eye on you. And if he don't, I shall. Ha ha."

He went on to reveal a life on the rolling waves. He had commanded a ship under Admiral Nelson, and declared that he would not live anywhere but on the coast, "not if you promised me a gold mine—or a tin mine. Ha ha." He touched his glass to mine and said, "A willing foe and sea room." I blinked to hear we were foes, on such short acquaintance. "Nelson's toast," he told me. "Many a bumper of rum I have enjoyed with him. The finest man who ever commanded a fleet, bar none."

Others accosted me as well. My fame had come before me, paving my way into the charmed circle. The only face that frowned on me was that of Lord Harelson, but as he gave everyone in the room the same rebukeful look, I did not take it personally. It rankled that Dalton had conned me about Grieve's dungeon, but I could forgive him, as I was making friends for the next season in London. At length we were called to dinner, and still no sign of our host!

When dinner was announced, I had the notion that Lord Harelson was propelling his frown in my direction. Lord Brockley beat him to it; snatched my elbow and said he would "pilot me through the shoals to a snug harbor," which he did.

Chapter Five

MR. DALTON WAS in the dining room when we entered, having gained access by some other route than via the saloon. He looked a pineapple of perfection in his evening clothes, nor did his table leave anything to be desired. The usual complement of silver, china, and crystal were on display, set off with a huge bouquet of garden flowers in the center. Seascape paintings hung on the wall. These were a little boring but infinitely preferable to the pictures of dead game that decorated Lorene's dining room, and were enough to turn you against your mutton. The food was good and plentiful, with perhaps more emphasis on fruits of the sea than I liked.

Dalton apologized to his guests for his late arrival, explaining that he had been detained by his man of business. I would not leave my guests waiting for the convenience of my man of business, but the assembled company smiled their understanding, and I did likewise. With such a surfeit of titles in the room, it was not to be expected that I sat within hollering distance of my host. We did no more than exchange a smile until after dinner, when the gentlemen had enjoyed their port and the ladies had enjoyed quizzing me about my fortune.

Dalton spoke to a few of the older ladies before wending his way to my chair, but I had the feeling from his first entry that I was his target, for he glanced at me several times. Our first conversation had to do with my trip to Brighton. Next was a question as to how I liked Lady Grieve's house.

"It is fine, if one enjoys living in a dungeon," I replied, with a sapient look.

"I offered to show you the house before you hired it."

"And I, like a fool, trusted your judgment. Odd you have not paneled your own house in dark oak, as you are so fond of it. I hope you did not put yourself to too much trouble convincing her ladyship to let me rent the place."

A trace of pink showed above his cravat, but he carried it off pretty well. "Caught in a snare of my own devising. It was a wretched thing to do; let us blame my eagerness for your company. There was nothing else vacant. Really it is not a bad house. I know for a fact that two other families were after it, which is why I was in such a rush to see Lady Grieve in London. The roof don't leak, the view is marvelous, and the gardens!"

His excuse was flattering enough to put me back in humor. "The deed is done. I have signed the contract, so I shall not give way to futile repinings."

"I hope the dinner party, at least, pleases you."

"Very nice. Now that I am aware of your sister's idea of meeting a few friends informally, I shall know how to behave if I am ever invited to a formal do. I shall rent Queen Charlotte's crown and buy a crimson velvet cloak."

He smiled to see me in good humor. "Tomorrow I shall show you the town—if you are free?"

"Shall we make it for the afternoon? I mean to tour the house and write up a list of things to have sent from London in the morning. I think that with a little effort, I can make the dungeon habitable. Lady Grieve won't mind if I store those cheap tourist things and take her fading prints to the attic?"

"She would have not objection if you painted the

dark oak, or installed new window hangings. She no longer uses the house, but has taken the idea it swells in value every day, so she is in no hurry to sell."

"I daresay she is right."

I had some more personal conversation for Mr. Dalton's ears, but it could wait for tomorrow. I meant to disillusion him regarding the extent of my fortune. Perhaps he, like Brockley and Collifer, believed me a nabob. I could not but wonder if that was why he was treating me so grandly. I also wondered how he knew I was a tin heiress. I had not told him.

No sooner had Mr. Dalton moved away than Lord Harelson brought his sneer to entertain me. "So you are Miss Denver," he said, in an uppity way that set my nerves on edge.

"And you, I collect, are Lord Harelson?"

"Just so."

"How nice for you," I said, in a manner imitating his own ennui.

"Nicer to be the elder son," he replied.

"Oh?"

"Harelson is my Christian name. It can be misleading."

This was of no possible interest to me, nor to any lady, unless she hoped to marry him. I assumed that Lady Filmore was aware of his status. "Where are you staying in Brighton, Lord Harelson?" I asked, for conversation's sake.

"In Papa's ugly old mansion on East Street, south of the pavilion. Papa used to be one of Prinny's set."

I asked about the princes's pavilion, and he described it in the most denigrating manner for five minutes. "I'll take you to see it, if you like," he said. I was amazed at the offer, coming from this sneering young nobleman.

"Very kind of you."

"May I call tomorrow and we shall arrange a time?"

It would be hard to say whether I was more surprised or displeased at the offer. "Mr. Dalton has promised to show me the town tomorrow afternoon."

"The morning, then?"

I could not like to offend Lady Filmore's special friend. Did he mean to bring her with him? If not, she might take a pet, and I was particularly anxious to keep in her good graces.

"Lady Filmore mentioned calling in the morning," I said. It was an outright lie, but I have never felt social lies counted for much.

"Another time, then. I shall pop in one of these days." On this cavalier speech, he rose and sauntered off, leaving me in confusion.

I soon concluded that the informal aspect of Lady Filmore's party meant she had provided no entertainment for after dinner. No one mentioned cards, or music, or dancing. Around eleven o'clock, the guests began to leave. Not wishing to hang on later than the rest, Hennie and I left, too. Lord Harelson had settled into a corner with a book, looking as if he meant to outsit us all. I could not think much of Lady Filmore's taste in beaux.

At home, Hennie and I settled in to discuss our outing. "Lord Harelson seems perpetually bored," I said.

"Lord Brockley hinted that you don't want to let him attach himself to you. Not the thing, he said."

"I cannot believe Mr. Dalton would let his sister go about with Harelson if there is anything wrong with him."

"I don't know just what Lord Brockley meant. He hadn't a good word to say about Lord Castlereagh or the Eldons either."

"Perhaps he is a Whig, and Harelson a Tory." I

mentioned that Mr. Dalton was driving us out to see Brighton tomorrow.

"Us, or you?" she asked archly.

"Why, I just assumed . . ."

"I shall be busy, but you go ahead, Eve," she said. "Lord Brockley offered to give me the tour."

"Aha! A beau!"

She turned pink as a peony and scoffed at the idea. We had a cup of cocoa and retired at eleven-thirty. It had been an enjoyable evening. Images from our busy day whirled around in my head as I lay in that strange bed, listening to the ocean rolling in. It sounded louder in the stillness of the night, but not too loud. I could become accustomed to it, with time.

A pleasant summer loomed before me—drives along the ocean, dinner parties, a few routs or assemblies, perhaps. Odd that with all the wonders of London, it was at little Brighton that I was beginning to find my social sea legs. I only hoped they would not be cut out from under me when the true size of my fortune was discovered. Thirty thousand was not contemptible by any means, but I had the vague feeling that these new acquaintances felt it was much more.

Lorene had not owned the tin mine outright. She was only a shareholder. While I had a larger fortune than many noble daughters, I had no grand family to enhance me. Just money was deemed rather vulgar. Some out-of-pocket minor nobleman might be happy to have me, but the world would know why he had married Miss Denver, from Cornwall. I did not intend to become a laughingstock in society, vulgarly buying myself a title.

In the morning, Hennie and I made a complete tour of the house, jotting down those items to be replaced. I itemized what I wished to be sent from London, and sent Tumble off in my carriage, as I would not need it that day. He was to stay overnight in London and return the next day. By eleven I was finished, and went out to inspect the garden.

I am no gardener, but certainly there were all sorts of beautiful flowers growing in profusion. The place was a regular bower of bliss, with a domed gazebo painted white in one corner, and a big enough lawn in the center to hold a table and chairs for my garden party. The gardener's name was Luke. He looked like a fox, with red hair, a pointy nose, and sly eyes. I found him bent over a berry patch, culling berries. He had a six-quart basket full and was not halfway along the patch yet.

"How nice! We shall have some of those for lunch!" I exclaimed. It occurred to me that the excess might make a nice thank-you present for Lady Filmore. I mentioned it to Luke.

He gave a sly smile, and began at once to talk about the roses. He was into a long speech about spraying against aphids when Hennie's head poked out the door and told me that Lady Filmore was here.

I hastened inside to make her welcome. She looked particularly lovely that day in a high poke bonnet and a pink sprigged muslin that would have looked ridiculous on anyone but Lady Filmore. It resembled something out of a children's book, with a wide ribbon at the waist and a great deal of bows and trim.

We brushed cheeks again. That seemed to be her standard greeting. I ordered tea, and we sat down to chat. Our first conversation was about her dinner party. She added a few details about some of the guests, but I felt her heart was not in it. Her blue eyes were shadowed, and her lips drooped.

"Is something the matter, Lady Filmore?" I asked gently.

Without further ado, she drew out a lace hankie

and applied it to her eyes. "It is Harelson," she sniffled.

"Mr. Dalton has turned him off?" I asked. This seemed the likeliest explanation, bearing in mind Lord Brockley's hint.

"No, it is not that Richard dislikes him. I have been seeing him for six months, more or less. I was sure he meant to marry me. I mean he even—he was most particular in his advances." She blushed up to her ears. I assumed she had allowed him certain intimacies that a lady only allows a prospective husband.

"Then what is the trouble?" I inquired.

"I don't think he loves me anymore," she said, and began bawling again. "I met Annabelle Monk in the shops this morning, and she said he had taken her to a picnic at St. Ann's Well yesterday afternoon. I had asked him to take me to the cemetery that afternoon—Mama is buried there, just by St. Nicholas Church, you know—and he told me he had to get his hair cut."

I patted her hand. "Perhaps you are as well off without him, Lady Filmore. He is only a younger son."

"I do not care for that!" she said angrily. "We would have plenty of blunt at least."

"You are fortunate to have been left well off," I said. I naturally assumed the late Lord Filmore had left her wealthy.

"I?" she said, staring with those big blue eyes, misted with tears. "Good gracious, I have not two pennies to rub together. Filmore left me destitute. He was a shocking bad manager. He lost my fortune and his own upon the 'change. I would not be battening myself on Richard if I had any money of my own, for he is very strict, considering I am not a deb. No, Harelson is well to grass, you must know. His papa is a wicked nipcheese, but some aunt left him a fortune."

"Well," I said, racking my brain for something to comfort her. "Gentlemen sometimes like to sow their oats before they settle down. Harelson is young yet, and so are you."

"I am practically twenty, Miss Denver," she said severely. I felt about a hundred and ten. "And Harelson is twenty-seven. I know he means to shab off on me."

This answered one question that had been puzzling me. I no longer thought that Lord Harelson meant to bring Lady Filmore when he called on me. I decided then and there I would not be home whenever he called. I did not care for him, and I certainly did not want to fall into Lady Filmore's bad books.

"Perhaps you have inadvertently offended him, in some manner," I said.

She sat, thinking about this in silence. At length I suggested we go into the garden, hoping the sunshine and flowers might be better for her than the unalleviated gloom of dark oak and dusty windows. I would set the servants to cleaning the windows that afternoon.

Luke had disappeared. I mentioned the strawberries to Lady Filmore, and she smiled her thanks. Unfortunately, Luke had not taken them to Cook, so I told her I would send them over when he returned. I also wondered where he was, when he should have been at work.

We chatted for half an hour, becoming better acquainted. I mentioned my alfresco party, and she smiled. "I shall wear my leghorn bonnet. I cannot wear it in the carriage, for it always blows off, and for walking, it is impossible."

This left me doubting whether I should also wear mine, for it was a dead replica of hers. We set on Saturday afternoon for the alfresco party.

"Be sure you invite Harelson," she said.

We were about to go inside when a gawky-looking

face peered over the hedge that shielded us from the street. "There you are!" the man exclaimed. "I have been looking for you next door, Linda."

"Stewart," she said, without either enthusiasm or annoyance.

He found the gate, and a new character entered my story.

Chapter Six

HIS NAME WAS Stewart Grindley, and despite his lack of either looks, talent, a title, or conversation, it seemed he was accepted in society. He was of middle height, somewhat stocky, wearing a blue jacket of good cut, but abominably wrinkled. His hair looked as if it had been hacked off with a carving knife and not seen a brush for twenty-four hours. His cravat had brownish spots on it, as of dropped tea. His rawboned, common face was redeemed from utter ugliness by a rather fine pair of brown eyes. Yet with all his sins, one sensed the gentleman lurking beneath. It was his utter lack of concern for his appearance that convinced me he was a gentleman. As Lady Filmore presented him to me as her friend, I had fresh tea made and brought out.

"Have you seen Harelson today, Stew?" she inquired, as soon as decently possible.

"Left at ten in his curricle. I was just waking up."

"Are you staying with Lord Harelson?" I asked, surprised that that bored nobleman would harbor Grindley under his roof.

"Hire a suite of rooms. Take breakfast there," Grindley replied. This went from bad to worse. Lord Harelson hiring out rooms? "Mean to say, nothing to let in Brighton. Lucky to get the dungeon, Miss Denver." He flopped his head, in an effort to toss a hank of hair out of his eyes. It tumbled back onto his forehead at once.

His omission of pronouns had a tendency to confuse, but this at least I could figure out. Obviously I was the fortunate one who had hired the dungeon.

"Are you a gambling lady?" was his next sally.

"No, I am not."

"Pity. Could put you on to a sure thing in the hurdle races. Betting a monkey on Blue Boy myself."

"You always lose, Stewart," Lady Filmore chided. "Will Harelson be attending the races with you?"

"Better. Mean to say, how am I to get there?" This time he used his hand to flop the hair back. "Sold up my curricle before leaving London. Came to town on the stage. Nicholson held the ribbons."

"Is Nicholson a friend of yours?" I asked, surprised that a gentleman would be on close terms with a stagecoach driver.

"At Oxford together," he replied, confusing me even further, but some sense eventually emerged. "For a golden boy, the stage driver will let you take the ribbons. Jolly good sport. Hadn't a golden boy to spare myself."

"When, exactly, is this hurdle race?" Lady Filmore asked. I knew why she was curious—Harelson would be there.

"Four o'clock today on the Hove."

"I shall take you in my carriage, Stewart," she said.

"Thankee kindly." Then he turned to me. "Remember, Blue Boy's your nag. Five to one. I'll place your bet, if you like."

"I do not gamble," I reminded him.

He stayed for fifteen minutes, during which time he continued the silent argument with the wayward lock of hair, and revealed that he was wearing one of Harelson's shirts, which was too small and pulled at his arms. Lady Filmore gave him the name of a local laundress to wash his linen. He seemed eager to avoid Lady Collifer, who I think was his aunt, but perhaps it was some other relationship. He complained of assorted noble relations. He was looking for a rich orphan, as his pockets were to let and he did not wish to acquire any more family.

Just before Lady Filmore removed him, he asked me how my parents were doing. I told him they were fine, thank you. If he had designs on this orphan's fortune, he was out in his luck.

"In Cornwall, are they?" he asked.

"Yes, as I have so many aunts and uncles and cousins in London, my parents trust me to their care."

"Pity."

Hennie sat with us, and if I have omitted her, it is because she did not take much part in the conversation, which left her free to listen with both ears.

"A fortune hunter!" she scoffed, when Grindley and Lady Filmore had left. "Lady Filmore has poor taste in gentlemen friends."

"She has eyes for no one but Lord Harelson. And he, in his own way, is as bad as Grindley. Imagine Harelson charging his friend rent, when he is supposed to be so rich."

"That's how they get rich," Hennie said. "Old Lord Stone in Cranbrook would skin a flea for the hide. They say he even sold his old clothes, and, of course, he sold the extra produce from his home garden, instead of leaving the extra for the servants."

This reminded me of the berries. I went after Luke, and found him in a little shed, counting out cardboard boxes. They were green, and would hold a quart of fruit. I asked him what had happened to the strawberries. He said Lady Grieve always gave the extra to the orphanage, and had instructed him to do likewise during her absence.

"That was before she hired the house out, Luke. For the duration of my tenancy, the fruit from this garden is mine. You will ask me before distributing it."

"You don't want to help out the poor orphans then, miss?" he said boldly.

"If I do, I shall let you know. Please pick another two quarts of berries this afternoon and take them to Mr. Dalton's cook. I have promised Lady Filmore some strawberries."

"There's no more ready to pick, miss. Tomorrow, maybe."

"I am sure you can find two more quarts, if you look."

"If you want to give them white and sour berries, or ones that the birds have got at . . ."

"Never mind," I said through tight lips, and went into the house to prepare for lunch. Dessert consisted of an extremely meager serving of strawberries. I hoped the orphans enjoyed their treat. I asked Mary Day to slip out and buy two quarts of strawberries and deliver them to Dalton's cook, as Lady Filmore had seemed pleased with the offer.

This recital of my morning may sound boring, but in fact, I reveled in having visitors, and even more in the prospect of driving out with Mr. Dalton that afternoon. When you have been left to your own devices for months, any little visit or outing assumes great importance. At one point last winter, Hennie had threatened to buy a parrot, just to have a new face to talk to. I hesitated for ten minutes over what outfit to wear, finally settling on the violet suit, the same one for which I had hoped to find an amethyst brooch at the pawnshop. The breeze from the sea could be chilly, and although Lady Filmore wore sprigged muslin, I feared Dalton might drive his open carriage.

When Mr. Dalton called, he was driving his curricle, so I felt I had dressed wisely. "Hennie is not able to come with us," I said.

Mr. Dalton was too well bred to show his pleasure, but a hint of it peeped out in his smile. We drove first along the seashore, past the fish market to the Hove, while Dalton explained that this was the south boundary of Brighton. Then he headed north and pointed out a few points of interest, ending up at the Prince's pavilion. That lovely folly is too well known to harp on, but it is just as marvelous as everyone says, with its lovely big dome and all sorts of lesser domes and minarets like something out of an Eastern fable. You half expect to see a flying carpet shoot out of a tower window.

"Lord Harelson offered to show me the pavilion," I mentioned, as I wished to bring this gentleman's name forward.

"His papa, Lord Comstock, used to be one of Prinny's set" was all he said.

"Do you think Lady Filmore will marry him?" was my next effort to draw him out.

"Perhaps, one day. She is young. There is no hurry."

"You would not object to the match?"

"It is hard to object to a gentleman of good birth and fortune and character," he replied. I did not sense any enthusiasm, but no real opposition either. It hardly seemed my place to quiz him further. Lady Filmore would tell him what she wished him to know.

We drove back toward the beach. Dalton suggested we alight for a walk along the shingles to enjoy the sea air. There were bathing machines with ladies and gentlemen taking a dip. I thought I might try it one day, but first I would have to have a proper bathing gown made up. They were exceedingly ugly, like long gray flannelette nightgowns.

Hawkers were selling ices and cold drinks. Dalton bought two ices, and we sat on a bench to enjoy them. "I would like to ask you something, Miss Denver," he said. His face was suddenly serious. Not only serious, but almost sheepish.

I knew this was not going to be a romantic something. That was not the way he looked. I sensed that it had to do with Harelson, and expressed the keenest interest.

"It is about that notice in the journals, of your coming to Brighton," he said.

"I have been wanting to speak to you about that, Mr. Dalton. I fear your friends overestimate my wealth. How did you know about the tin mine, and Cornwall?"

"I took the trouble to find out who you are, after you dropped that stolen ring in my pocket." That took the wind out of my sails entirely. I considered denying it, but his knowing eyes made a mockery of that notion.

"How did you find out about me? I don't know your set."

"Your man of business, Mr. Foster, knows many people. He knows my man of business. That is how I found out. There are not that many heiresses on the town that your secret is safe, no matter how closely you tried to guard it."

I sat like a mute, not disabusing him of the notion that I had voluntarily consigned myself to anonymity. "I see," I said. "I expect you know the extent of my fortune?"

"I do, and it is an impressive size. Too large for you to be stealing rings. I assumed, therefore, that you were telling me the truth about how you came by the emerald."

"Of course I was telling the truth! Do you take me for a common thief?"

"No, a very uncommon one," he said, and laughed. "And if society overestimates your fortune, then you are in vogue with the rest of the heiresses. One automatically cuts every fortune rumor in half, then in half again, to get at an idea of the true size."

"What was it you wished to discuss then? I took the ring in a moment's pique when I discovered Parker's stunt with my diamond. I did drop the ring in your pocket. It was a horrid thing to do, but I was afraid I would be arrested and found with the thing in my pocket. You knew it was there all along?"

"Certainly. I discovered it not ten minutes later, and soon figured out how it had got there. I thought I would have to loiter about at Shepherd's Market to find you again. You may imagine my joy at seeing you in Hyde Park later that day."

"So you lied to me, too," I pointed out.

"One good lie deserves another. I had not yet discovered your identity. I followed you to South Audley Street, and went from there directly to my man of business. When I learned you were a lady of good reputation and considerable property, I felt you would do the proper thing, and return Lady Dormere's ring to her. Which you did—eventually." A mischievous smile reminded me of my reluctance to do so.

"If I hesitated, it is only that I had no reason to trust you. I knew that ring had not fallen out of your pocket. I thought you were planning to keep it."

"I know you did. I should resent it, but as I wronged you, I withhold my resentment. Isn't it nice that we now know we are both above reproach?"

"I am glad the air is cleared. I am not used to deceit."

He cocked his head to one side. "Pity. I was about to suggest a whole summer of deceit to you, Miss Denver."

"Indeed! And what form would this summer of deceit take?"

"I happen to require an heiress to act as bait to catch Tom, the burglar. If common gossip toots you as a fabulous heiress, you will be a natural target for him, as you suggested yourself."

"You have brought me here to lure a burglar! You have shouted in the journals that I am rich, and put me into Lady Grieve's dungeon, for the purpose of having my jewels stolen? Well, upon my word, Mr. Dalton. You go too far!"

"No, no. I brought you here for the purpose of catching Tom. Naturally your jewels, if you have any troublesome amount of them, will be safely sequestered elsewhere."

"As a matter of fact, I do have rather a lot of jewelry." I explained about my stepmama's taking her friends' jewelry as collateral.

"Best get them into a safety box at the bank at once."

I was intrigued by Dalton's plan and asked what my part in it would be.

"You would have to become more highly visible than you will like. That is all. Go about in society, wearing your jewels. Your name would appear in the journals, relating your doings. In short, I am asking you to become one of society's outstanding ladies of fashion, to attract Tom's attention."

Dalton regarded me fearfully, thinking I would cry out in horror at becoming a public figure. I was thrilled to death, but, of course, did not say so. "It sounds tedious," I said doubtfully. "Why is it your job to catch Tom, Mr. Dalton?"

"Because he robbed me of five hundred pounds, and several of my friends of jewelry. Bow Street is active in the case, of course, but Townshend thinks the thief is a member of society. Some gent down on his luck—or lady, for that matter," he added. "They have asked me to help. I consider it my duty to help uphold the law," he said nobly. Then he added with a twinkle, "Besides, it is demmed good fun pitting my wits against Tom."

"Despite what you know of me, I, too, am eager to uphold the law. Just one thing puzzles me." He looked interested. "Why did you pick on me, when you know any number of ladies who are already well-known society figures?"

"There are several reasons. The idea came to me when I discovered how brave and quick-thinking you are. I refer to your lifting the emerald ring, and dumping it in my pocket when the constable came on the scene. Then, too, it was my hope that my accomplice would agree to live in Lady Grieve's dungeon, close by, for easy communication. I preferred a younger lady—and that you happened to be attractive was no deterrent." A glance full of admiration darted all over me. "There, I have opened my budget. Will you do it?"

"At some point in this summer of deceit, am I likely to end up with Tom's gun pointing at my nose? I fear that going to bed every night with the fear of having Tom invade my house will deprive me of my beauty sleep."

"I cannot say there is no danger in it, but there is not so much as you fear. Tom never strikes when the victim is at home. He seems to have ways of knowing when his victim is out, which is why Townshend feels he is a member of society, aware of such things. I want to make all your doings public knowledge, so that it will not look unusual if the journals announce you are off visiting this or that castle for a weekend. Tom will not strike until he has had time to gauge your jewels, which is why I want you to wear them on every outing. He will strike in a couple of weeks, and while he knows you are away. And I shall be there, waiting for him. Indeed, I have already hired a man to watch your house from dusk till dawn. Tom will soon hear of you. Already the folks who met you last night at my house are bruiting your presence about town."

"That is why you invited me," I said, not wholly feigning my annoyance.

"That is one reason. It is not good for a lady to be without friends. I fear your self-imposed isolation is turning you cranky," he said, with a bold smile. "I also would like Linda to have a good, sensible lady friend. And as I implied earlier, I have no aversion to a pretty neighbor myself."

"It seems to me you have set me up as Tom's target whether I like it or not. It would be foolish to refuse your help, as he will certainly have a go at my jewels in any case."

"A word whispered in the right ears will return you to anonymity, if that is what you wish," he said. "I have only to hint that Miss Denver is not so well to grass as I thought, and you will not be troubled by Tom or anyone else. In fact, if you dislike the scheme, I shall happily refund you the rent of the house and let you return to London, for I would like to plant someone in there this summer, to help me catch Tom."

"But I am enjoying Brighton! I do not want to leave. I'll do it," I said, before he could say any more about anonymity, or leaving.

"God bless you, Miss Denver. I shall be eternally in your debt. Now, this evening, I would like you to put on your diamonds and come to a gaming hell with me."

"Mr. Dalton!"

"Mrs. Lamont's gaming hell is all the crack this year," he said blandly. "We shall drop in around midnight, after Lady Verona Shelby's rout. I shall call for you and Mrs. Henderson around nine, if that suits you? Perhaps your aunt will want to skip the gaming hell."

I was overcome with a fit of giggles, like a green girl. I never thought I would be one of the charmed circle, darting wildly from routs to gaming hells, with a handsome escort like Mr. Dalton. I fear I must desist from drawing a moral here, or you will take the notion that stealing is the way to get what you want. Still, there is no denying that if I had not stolen Lady Dormere's emerald ring, I would still be sitting at home alone in London, while some other lady acted as bait for Tom.

Chapter Seven

"WILL THESE STRAWBERRIES do, Mum?" Mary asked, when I went to speak to Cook about dinner. She showed me two quarts of perfect, ruby red berries, resting in familiar green boxes.

"They look fine, Mary. Take them next door, with my compliments."

"The greengrocer told me as how the best berries always come from Lady Grieve's garden," Mary said, and tittered.

"I suspected as much. What did you pay for them?" She told me, and I said, "Call Luke in, Mary, if you please."

I heard her jawing at him as they approached. "You're for it now, mister. She's got a rare temper when you set her off."

Luke entered, somewhat chastened, but still with that sly fox look on his face. "The twelve quarts of berries you sold to the greengrocer will be deducted from your wage, Luke." I purposely named a larger amount than I thought he had taken. When he did not object, I assumed he had stolen more than a dozen. "I will not tolerate pilfering. In future, I wish to know how much produce is culled from the garden. *I* shall decide what to do with it. The greengrocer is not my favorite charity. If this occurs again, I shall notify Lady Grieve. That is all."

"The extra produce is part of my wage when Lady Grieve is here," he said with a sulky look.

"Don't try to con me, you sly rogue. She has not

been here for decades. Now go, before I box your ears."

He left, without even apologizing, and I went to tell Hennie the news about our being bait for Tom.

"Are you crazy?" she demanded. "You'll lose all your jewels. We shall be fortunate if he don't slit our throats."

I explained how the thing would work, and she settled down to a dull grumble. To rouse her out of the sulks, I told her about Lady Verona Shelby's rout, adding that I would go on to another do with Mr. Dalton.

"What is this other do? Perhaps I would like to go along to it as well."

"It is a gaming hell, Hennie, and you are perfectly welcome to come along, if you wish."

Her eyes opened up like saucers. "A gaming hell! I don't know what the vicar would say."

"Yes, you do. David would say it was a den of the devil," I teased, and left, hoping she would not accompany us.

Until dinnertime, I planned my garden party for Saturday afternoon. Thus far, I had not made many acquaintances, but I meant to invite everyone I had met, including even Stewart Grindley. One other duty that had to be taken care of very soon was the matter of additions to my toilette. I would ask Lady Filmore to recommend a modiste to me. Her advice would be invaluable, as she always turned out in the first style of fashion. It was a good way for us to further our acquaintance.

I was not entirely without handsome gowns, however, and for that evening I wore a green one the shade of tulip leaves, edged with silver lace and ribbons. With it, I wore Lorene's diamond necklace and carried a lace shawl. This latter article offered more style than warmth. Hennie squinted her eyes at it and said, "I have heard the road to hell is paved with vanity."

"You have heard wrong. It is paved with good intentions."

When Mr. Dalton called for us, he had Lady Filmore along with him, resplendent as usual, this time in a cream-colored gown with sapphires as lovely as her eyes. During the drive to Lady Verona's on German Place, I asked Lady Filmore's advice on a modiste, and she offered to accompany me the next morning to her Frenchwoman on Paradise Street, near All Souls Church.

All the people I had met at Mr. Dalton's dinner party were at Lady Verona's, and a great many more besides. The ones I had met greeted me as an old friend. My first partner was Mr. Dalton, who danced with grace and charm. At the dance's end, there was a crush of beaux lined up to meet me. I felt as courted as Prinny's heir, Princess Charlotte. I had to remind myself that Mr. Dalton could return me to anonymity with a word, or my head would have grown too large to carry. Of course, it was my dot these fellows were interested in, but they had to take me along with it, and that was good enough for the nonce.

I invited half the people there to my garden party on Saturday. Ladies and gentlemen, young and old, if they looked halfway respectable, I invited them. Not one soul refused either. I can say without boasting that my projected party was the on-dit of the evening.

It was for the fifth set that Lord Harelson wedged his way through the throng and asked me to stand up with him.

"I hear you are having a little do Saturday," he said. A surprising number of my partners used that opening ploy. In his case it was unnecessary.

"Lady Filmore has most particularly told me I must invite you," I said. "I hope you can come."

"Ah, Linda will be there, will she?"

"Of course."

"Well, I shall come anyhow."

"I thought that might induce you," I said, looking a question at his lack of enthusiasm.

"No, Miss Denver, *that* is not what induces me," he said, with a smile. He could be quite charming, when he roused himself out of his usual torpor. I began to see what Lady Filmore had seen in him.

That smile made me realize that Harelson had an eye on me himself. It was an extremely touchy state of affairs. "Just so long as you come," I said, and turned the conversation to Stewart Grindley. If that name did not kill his flirtatious mood, I don't know what would.

"Grindley said he had met you. He is putting up with me for the summer. Deuced odd fellow. He insists on paying rent, as if I were running an inn. I only take it to have some cash on hand to lend him when his pockets are to let. I don't mind having him about, but I wish he would wear his own shirts."

"Did his nag win the hurdle races? He seemed to put great faith in a horse called Blue Boy."

"Blue Boy trailed the field. You never want to put your blunt on any nag Grindley recommends. Now, if you are a betting lady, I can—"

"Oh no. I am not interested in that, Lord Harelson."

The dance was pleasant enough. His flirtation never exceeded the bounds of good taste. Before leaving, he mentioned that he would "pop in" to see me, sometime he was in the neighborhood. I assented without undue enthusiasm.

Just before dinner I went abovestairs to tidy myself, and met Hennie there, rouging her cheeks. Now, the late vicar, you must know, had no opinion of rouge.

"Paving the road to hell, are you, Hennie!" I quizzed. "Where did you get that?"

"From your toilet table at home," she retorted,

squinting at me. "Lord Brockley asked me if I was feeling faint. I felt fine, and concluded I must be too pale. I have decided to buy a pot of rouge, Eve. Every lady here over thirty is painted—and a few of them who are younger than that." This was a jibe at my occasional use of rouge. I was not wearing it that evening. "Why should *I* look like a flat?"

"Why indeed? Here, let me smooth in the edges for you." She had it sitting in two circles, low on her cheeks. "Have you decided about coming on to Mrs. Lamont's gaming hell later?"

"I shall be going, but not with you and the Daltons. Lord Brockley is taking me. I don't suppose you could lend me a couple of shillings, Eve? I did not bring any money with me."

"A couple of shillings will not get you far. Here, take this," I said, and gave her a couple of guineas.

"Good gracious! I don't mean to dip so deeply as that."

But she took the money, and tucked it into her little beaded reticule. Hennie looked pretty that evening. Her eyes sparkled with a new light, and the rouge became her.

"Are you setting up a flirtation with Lord Brockley, Auntie?" I teased.

"No, he is trying to set up one with me. He is a widower."

"I knew he was available. I thought he was a bachelor."

"No, his wife died a decade ago. He finds it lonesome without her. His kiddies are all grown-up."

Lady Filmore and some other ladies came in just as we were about to leave. "Miss Denver, could I speak to you for a moment?" Lady Filmore asked, drawing me off to a corner. "I saw you dancing with Harelson. Did he say anything about me?"

"I told him you would be at my garden party, and he was eager to come."

"What did he say?" she asked, with pathetic eagerness. It seemed unkind to lead her on, but if the fellow planned to jilt her, I saw no reason why I should be his messenger.

"He said he looked forward to it."

"Is he going on to Mrs. Lamont's after the rout tonight?"

"He did not mention it."

"He will surely be there. I shall go with you and Richard. You don't mind?"

"Good gracious, no. Why should I mind?"

She gave me a knowing smile. "I thought you two might want to be alone. I have never seen Richard so mad about a lady for months. He quite dotes on you, Miss Denver."

"There is nothing like that between us, Lady Filmore," I expostulated. I was about to mention the true nature of our dealings, when it struck me that Dalton might not want her to know. She was a flighty little thing; she might unwittingly give the secret away.

"And birds do not have wings either." She smiled.

Hennie was waiting by the door, so I joined her, and we went down to dinner. I sat with Mr. Dalton, and while we ate, I asked whether his sister was aware of our plan to trap Tom.

"She knows I am working with Townshend. I did not tell her that you are involved. You have not mentioned it to anyone?"

"I am not a flat! I did not even tell Lady Filmore."

"Good. It is more than likely that Tom is sitting in this room. Possibly right at this table."

Lady Verona had four round tables set up in her dining room. At ours, most of the same people from Dalton's dinner party sat. I supposed they were good friends, and tended to gather together at such dos as this. Lady Collifer and her husband were there; Hennie and Lord Brockley; Lady Filmore had managed to get Harelson to sit with her. There were eighteen in all. Mr. Grindley was there, with some hatchet-faced lady in a straw yellow gown, the same shade as her face. Surely this was not the group Dalton meant when he suggested that Tom might be one of us. They all, with the exception of Stewart Grindley, looked above reproach. Several of them had titles. I pictured Tom as more of an outsider, someone who had weaseled his way into the golden circle to ferret out news of their doings. I had not met anyone like that—except possibly Grindley?

We left for Mrs. Lamont's gaming hell shortly after dinner. If I had not known gaming dens to be infra dig, I would not have twigged to it by either the looks of the house, nor the guests. Everything was done up in the first style of elegance. Several of Lady Verona's guests showed up, and the others looked equally respectable. Dalton took up a seat at the faro table, and Lady Filmore and myself, who were tyros at gambling, stood at the roulette table, putting down our chips and having them pulled away at every turn of the wheel.

Lady Filmore played the more daring game. She bet on the actual numbers. I settled for red or black and lost my blunt at a slower rate, but equally surely.

"There, my pockets are to let. I have lost twenty guineas," Lady Filmore said, after half an hour. "Dalton will cut up stiff. The skint only gave me twenty guineas."

Twenty guineas sounded like a great loss to me, but I smiled gamely and suggested we take a seat and have a glass of champagne, to rest our legs. As the wine was free, I meant to recoup part of my five guineas in liquid form. Lady Filmore took one sip, then set her glass aside, wrinkling up her nose. There was certainly a hint of vinegar to the wine, but I was thirsty, and finished mine. Mrs. Lamont served little tidbits of salted nuts and olives and things with it.

I kept an eye on the others while I drank. Dalton was playing faro with an air almost of ennui. At the roulette table, Hennie placed her bets with the fevered eye of the tyro. Lady Filmore was watching Harelson in that peculiarly proprietary way she has. He was plunging rather deeply, but when he joined us later, he claimed he was even steven.

He asked if we had seen Grindley, which we had not. "I was to meet him here, but he is late," he said. "Just as well, really. Mrs. Lamont would let him punt on tick. I know for a fact he is stone broke. He would end up selling his carriage and team and be forever borrowing mine. He has already sold his curricle. And how did you fare at the table, Miss Denver?"

"I lost."

"Try again. Your luck is bound to change."

"I am fresh out of money," I explained.

"Good God, Mrs. Lamont will give you credit—a lady with your fortune at her back."

"I fear that fortune would not be there long if I gambled further, Lord Harelson."

"Unlucky at cards, lucky at love," he said, with a smile as warm as it dared to be in front of Lady Filmore. Then he turned to her. "How about you, Linda? Are you interested in trying faro?" I sensed he was eager to return to his gambling.

She hopped up at once, and they left. Lady Collifer joined me, lamenting that she had lost a monkey, and would never come again if the only food served was to be nuts and olives. Have I mentioned she was a corpulent lady? A fine trencherman.

After another glass of champagne, Hennie joined us, smiling from ear to ear. "I won twelve pounds, Eve!" she exclaimed. "Here is the two I borrowed from you. Take them before I lose them again. Lord Brockley is teaching me to play roulette. The trick is to bet the numbers. You don't make enough to bother with on the colors."

"But the odds are not so high against you," I pointed out.

"The gaming table is no place for the faint-hearted," she informed me.

The vicar's widow was sliding fast down the slippery road to damnation. Only last week she had refused to buy a raffle ticket, and that was for charity. She swilled down a glass of champagne and trotted back to the roulette table. I hoped Lord Brockley would not introduce her to the vice of punting on tick when she had lost her ten pounds.

We did not remain long at Mrs. Lamont's. Mr. Dalton refused to reveal how much he had lost, which inclined me to think it was a large sum. We dropped Lady Filmore off at her front door, and Mr. Dalton walked me home.

A fat white moon shone above, casting shimmering ripples of gold and silver on the ocean's face. A breeze lifted my lace shawl. I shivered, but whether it was the wind or the handsome face lurking in romantic shadows above me that caused it, I could not say.

Chapter Eight

"Did you enjoy your evening?" Mr. Dalton asked.

"I enjoyed the rout, but gambling is boring," I told him, to prevent a repeat engagement. "If I want to gamble, I would prefer to play cards, where some skill is involved."

"We don't have to go back. I wanted you to be seen by more people. The sooner you are known, the faster we catch Tom."

I had hoped for a more personal sort of conversation, but did not mean to institute it myself. "Do you think it possible Grindley might be involved?" I suggested. "He has no money; he gambles; he has managed somehow to be a part of society."

"I have pinned my suspicions on a dozen people, over the months. My feeling is that Tom has got money from his thievery, which is why I tend to discount Grindley. Besides, Grindley is an awkward concern. I cannot see him scampering up a trellis and sneaking into a lady's chamber without breaking the window or knocking over a chair. But I fancy it is someone like him. Some young buck who has run through his own fortune."

"His awkwardness could be an act to avoid suspicion, and so could his poverty. I mean Tom might be amassing a fortune, planning to skip off abroad when he feels he has enough. Or he might be losing the money as fast as he steals it. Grindley is an unlucky gambler—horse races, the gaming table."

"I don't count anyone out," he said.

We were at the door. As it was one o'clock in the morning and I did not know whether Hennie was home yet, I did not invite him in. He thanked me for the strawberries; I told him he was welcome. I did not tell him their history, as I was ashamed of being duped by my own gardener.

"I shall call on you tomorrow to arrange the evening's outing. You are still game?"

"Certainly. I do not welsh on my bargains, Mr. Dalton."

"And about your jewelry—we want to get it out of your house soon, for safety's sake."

"If I am to continue wearing it, then it will be awkward to have it in a bank."

"I had a safe installed at my place after I was robbed, and my servants are always on guard. What do you think of leaving it with me? It would be handy for your use."

"That sounds a good idea. Do you want to take it tonight?"

"Do you have it put away safely?"

"It is hidden under my mattress."

He shook his head and *tsk*ed at my simplicity. "And here I thought you were up to all the rigs, Miss Denver. That is the first place Tom would look. Put it at the bottom of your potato barrel tonight, and I shall collect it tomorrow."

"I will do nothing of the sort. I am not going into the cellar alone at this hour of the night. Tumble does not return from London until tomorrow. I sent him to get some decent furnishings. I told the servants to lock the doors and leave one light on downstairs."

"I don't like to send a lady alone into a house at night. I shall go with you and collect your jewelry while we are about it."

I hesitated a moment, wondering if I was quite safe alone with Mr. Dalton. I feared I was, but a little maidenly reluctance seemed called for. His eyes opened wide in amusement. "Surely you are not afraid of me!" he exclaimed. "I would never take advantage of a lady."

"That has not been my experience, sir! You bullocked me into this scheme in the first place," I replied playfully. Then I slipped the key into the lock and opened the door, before he could remind me how that had come about.

I lit a few lamps, as the dark-paneled room looked like a grotto, with only one feeble light burning. "Help yourself to a glass of wine, while I go and root the jewels out from under the mattress."

I nipped smartly upstairs, got out the jewel box, and returned to the saloon. Mr. Dalton had poured two glasses of wine. He began to rise from the sofa when I entered, but I motioned him to remain seated, and joined him.

I opened the large, varnished box that held Lorene's jewelry. It was lined in blue satin, with little pockets to hold her treasures. I never really gave much thought to the collection. A deal of it was made up of her "collaterals," old-fashioned diamond rings, two diamond bracelets, and a clutter of jeweled brooches. Her own jewelry was more valuable. Besides the diamonds I was wearing, there was a long rope of good pearls and an intricate jeweled necklace of rubies, sapphires, and diamonds, which always reminded me of our flag. It was not very pretty, but some of the gemstones were large and no doubt valuable. There was another diamond and emerald necklace with matching bracelet, and several rings of various precious stones.

"Good Lord!" Dalton exclaimed, when he looked at it. "You have a king's ransom here! It is well you laid low, Miss Denver. If Tom had learned of this . . ." He lifted out the pearls. They swung from his fingers, glowing in the lamplight.

"These would goad him into action, if he knew of them."

"He soon will. Tomorrow evening I want you to wear these," he said, holding the pearls against my gown. "Marvelous. Where did Lorene find such a treasure?" It sounded strange, to hear the name "Lorene" drop so familiarly from his lips.

"Her papa was a nabob. I believe these went to India via the Gulf of Persia."

"There is a tint almost of pink to them. If you ever want to sell this, I would be interested in purchasing it."

"I do not plan to frequent the gaming hells, so it should not be necessary for me to sell it."

"May I ask you a personal question?" I nodded and he said, "How did you come to hawk your chipped diamond ring?"

"It was Lord Hutching's satinwood commode that caused it. I paid cash, forgetting that my bank account was low. It was only for a few days, till some bonds came due."

He shook his head at such an unbusinesslike way of carrying on. We examined some of the other pieces. Our hands brushed from time to time, but true to his word, Dalton did not take advantage of the intimacy to misbehave. He suggested that we make an inventory of the merchandise.

"I trust you, Mr. Dalton," I said. I did not add that I had a good memory for what was in the box.

"Perhaps you are too trusting, Miss Denver," he murmured, gazing at me bemusedly. The air began to crackle.

Before more could be said, the door opened and Hennie came barging in, alone. Lord Brockley had left her at the door.

"Eve, what are you doing alone with a man at this hour of the night!" was her greeting. Then her beady little eyes spotted the jewel box. "What is that doing down here?" she inquired, in a tone of lively suspicion.

"Mr. Dalton is going to take it for safekeeping. He has a safe in his house."

Next she spotted the wineglasses, and her breathing became noticeably labored. "I would like to have a word with you when Mr. Dalton leaves," she said. Her tone suggested that he would be wise not to linger.

I noticed him chewing back a smile, and was relieved he had not taken offense. He rose at once to take his leave. "We shall be in touch tomorrow, Miss Denver. Good evening, ladies." He made an exquisite bow, and left.

"I think you have lost your wits, entertaining a gentleman alone at such an hour!" Hennie exclaimed.

"And who, may I inquire, was playing propriety with you and Lord Brockley until one-thirty in the morning?"

"I am an old lady, well past such things."

"What things, Hennie?" I teased. "Mr. Dalton came to pick up my jewelry for safekeeping."

"So he says. We don't know a thing about the fellow but what he chooses to tell us. You may never see those things again, or like Mrs. Minton's ring, they will come back wearing glass stones."

I felt a perfect fool. I had been so worried what Mr. Dalton's opinion of me that I never gave a thought to my opinion of him.

"What was he doing loitering outside of Parker's shop in the first place?" she continued. "Who is to say he was not waiting for a quiet minute to slip in and sell his stolen wares? Remember how sly he was about pretending he could not find the emerald ring? There are strange kinks in that lad."

"Don't be ridiculous. He is top of the trees."

"Aye, but who *is* he? He does not have a handle to his name, does he?"

"I fear Lord Brockley's handle has gone to your simple head. I am going to bed now, Hennie. I suggest you remove your rouge and do the same. And the next time I invite a gentleman into this house, I would prefer if you not insult him." I rose, bristling with dignity, to hide my concern. "Did you lose your ten pounds?" I asked.

"Yes, and I am glad I did. It has cured me of gambling. Ten pounds whistled down the wind inside of thirty minutes. Let it be a lesson to us. A fool and her money . . ."

"I am going to visit the modiste with Lady Filmore tomorrow morning. You are welcome to come with us, if you wish."

"I shall be driving out with Lord Brockley," she announced, and poured herself a glass of wine.

Hennie never had wine before going to bed. Had I perverted her, as well as myself, with this hankering for society?

I took my worries upstairs with me. I thought of my box of jewels, handed over to Mr. Dalton without so much as a receipt. I went to the side window to see if I could spot the man he said he had guarding my house. There was not a sign of him. I looked at Dalton's house. Only the rear of it was visible behind an old yew hedge. There were lights on in one room. Was he even now prying out the diamonds and rubies and sapphires? Weighing my pearls, which had so entranced him. Planning how he would replace them with fish paste. Well, he could not achieve it in one night, and tomorrow I would certainly demand the whole collection back. I was a fool to have trusted a stranger, and one whose behavior, when exposed to the clear light of reason, was questionable on many points.

Who was to say Dalton was not Tom himself, running a new rig since society must have taken precautions against him by now? He had no shortage of money, nor had he ever mentioned how he came by his fortune. I was easy pickings for him—a greenhead with a large fortune, and no family or close friends to guide her. He knew exactly how I was situated, too. Foster was familiar with my background, and he had access to Foster.

Between my worries and the surf pounding, I really did not need the pair of amorous felines who took to caterwauling outside my window that night. They were at it till all hours, uttering the most unabashed sounds, as they wallowed in animal ecstacy. At three o'clock I opened the window and threw my silver evening slippers at them. There was one louder meow than before, then a rustle of grass and finally blessed silence. Except, of course, for the demmed surf pounding. A wind had arisen, and trees took to whipping around.

I saw by a streak of lightning that the clock said three-fifteen; then I put my head under the pillow and finally slept.

Chapter Nine

My sleepless night left me cranky and hagridden. Hennie, on the other hand, had rejuvenated to girlhood. When she asked if she might borrow one of my bonnets, I knew she was halfway in love with Lord Brockley. I had been trying for an age to give her a new bonnet, but she always suggested I give the money to charity, if I had more than I knew what to do with. My only consolation was that Lady Filmore, when she stopped for me, looked nearly as hagged as I.

"What are your slippers doing in the front yard, Miss Denver?" she asked.

"I threw them at those cats that were making such a racket last night," I admitted, and sent Mary out to retrieve them.

"Good. I wondered why they suddenly stopped howling."

This told me that she had not slept well either. Lord Harelson, I thought, was what had kept her awake.

As soon as we were in her carriage, I said, "I hope you and Harelson patched up your quarrel last night?"

"No, Mrs. Lamont's was too public a place for that. I asked him to drive me home, but he said he was to meet Grindley at Mrs. Lamont's later, so he could not come. He will call this afternoon if he does not go to Eastbourne to see his friend."

We spent over an hour at Mrs. Drouin's shop on

Paradise Street. I had to be measured, as I was a new client. The French modiste treated me like royalty, when I came under Lady Filmore's auspices. My voice never rose above a polite murmur, which is not its customary volume when I am in the hands of a modiste. I ordered three gowns, and meant to return to have some new clothes made up for winter as well. She was awaiting a shipment of silks that were being smuggled in from France. Her workmanship was of the finest, and her patterns all from France. Lady Filmore ordered a blue mulled muslin, a replica of a pink mulled muslin she had bought the year before.

From there we drove to the milliner's. "I must have a new bonnet for your garden party, whatever Richard says," she pouted. "He is forever nagging at me for spending too much money. I declare, Miss Denver, I might as well be married, for he is as bad as a husband."

I did not try to talk her out of a new bonnet. I could now wear my replica of her leghorn, the one she wears in her portrait at Somerset House, without fearing duplication. Her choice was a glazed straw with blue ribbons that tied under the chin. She looked so pretty in it, I don't know how Harelson could help falling in love with her.

It was enjoyable, strolling through the shops with another young lady, especially as I had not left Hennie alone. It was good for us to get away from each other now and then. Being too much together is bound to grate on the nerves. I met a good many new people that morning. Lady Filmore was the darling of the ton, and I was accepted as her friend. Nearly everyone we met asked for Mr. Dalton. In the clear light of day, it seemed impossible to believe that such a well-established gentleman was trying to steal my jewels. Lady Filmore did not mention my having entrusted them to him, and as I was unsure whether he wished her to know, I did not mention it either, but it was often on my mind during that otherwise delightful morning.

Hennie invited Lord Brockley to join us for luncheon. That was enjoyable, too. Not that his conversation added much of interest, but I was happy for Hennie's sake. He looked rather odd, all decked out in gray, from head to toe. Other than the color, his jacket and trousers were of the conventional cut. His conversation was peppered with the names of the great, even including the Prince of Wales.

"Brighton is not what it was used to be," he said. "We had great times here in the old days. Coursing hares, hunting. That was before it got built up. We once hunted a carted stag all the way from the Steyne to Rottingdean. And of course, sailing and bathing, and all manner of mischief after dark. Prinny and Mrs. FitzHerbert—ah, 'tis a pity he ever left her. He was used to stay at Grove House in those days. Drove down from London in a post chaise to show his people how economical he was. Mrs. FitzHerbert had hired a house behind the Castle Inn, right at his back door. It lent an aura of intrigue, all the slipping around. Of course, everyone and his dog knew what was going on. The crowds trailed after them everywhere they went. She was a handsome lady in her youth. Hair as yellow as corn. The nose a bit hooked, but a handsome lady withal.

"That was before I went to sea. There is no fun at the pavilion nowadays, but if you ladies would like to see it, I shall take you to call, just to give you a look at it."

We both expressed pleasure at this rare treat. With some concern for Dalton's reputation, I dropped a few hints as to how long he had known Mr. Dalton.

"I have known him forever," he said. "The Daltons are a fine old Somerset family. They send two members up to Parliament. The family seat is called

Gracemere—a lovely old Tudor castle, but all built up in other styles over the years. Richard, your neighbor, is the only son. He has made a fortune in investments. Of course, he did not start from the ground by a long shot. Always very well to grass, the Daltons."

This recital calmed my fears for my jewels. Hennie took her beau out to see the garden before he left. No sooner were they out the door than Mr. Dalton came pelting in. "Have you heard?" he asked, his eyes wide open.

I thought the prince must have died, or Boney escaped again, or something equally horrid. "What is it?" I demanded, clutching my heart.

"Tom has struck again. He got away with a fine haul from Lady Harkness. She had most of her jewelry in a safety box, but, like myself, she had a sum of cash in her desk. A thousand pounds, I have heard mentioned."

"Good God! When did it happen?"

"That is the deuce of it; she don't know. She brought the money down with her a week ago from London and only went to take some out to pay her bills this morning. The box was empty. She was out two or three nights. In fact, she was at Lady Verona's party just last evening. The servants were at home and heard nothing."

"Is it possible the servants took it?"

"She has known them forever. She vouches for their honesty. No, it sounds like Tom's work. My own feeling is that it happened just last night. Officer Hutton, the constable, says the library door had been pried open. One would think someone would have noticed sooner if it happened before last night, although it seems the library is not much used. No one remembers having been in it yesterday, so I daresay it might have happened the night before last. I have sent a message off to Bow Street.

Townshend will want to have an officer here if Tom has removed to Brighton."

"Is my jewelry safe, Mr. Dalton?"

"Yes, I checked it the moment I heard of this latest robbery."

This gave me pause about asking for it back. Lord Brockley had vouched for Dalton. He and his sister were society's darlings, and now he had sent off for Bow Street. Surely this was not the behavior of a thief. And besides, I had no such safe place to keep it here as he had at his house. The bank was an alternative, of course, but one does not like to have to drive to the bank every time she wants to wear a necklace.

He watched me closely, sensing my doubts, though not, I trust, the exact nature of them. "The decision is yours, of course, but I do feel your valuables are as safe at my house as in the bank, and a deal more convenient. Tom, like lightning, does not seem to strike the same place twice, and he has already robbed me."

"I suppose you are right."

"If you fear losing them all, you could place half of them in a bank safe. Then if either the bank or my house is hit, you will still have something to wear. In any case, you will get your money back. The things are insured, of course?"

"No, I never bothered with that."

His mouth fell open. He swallowed a couple of times and said in a weak voice, "I suggest you insure them at once."

"Perhaps you are right," I agreed. Then if, by any chance, Mr. Dalton's first name was Tom, I would still get my money back. "I shall speak to an agent this very afternoon."

"Best not to waste a minute. He will want to examine the merchandise. Feel free to bring him to my house. Linda will be out this afternoon, so—"

"Ah, I meant to ask if she knew you had my things. I did not mention it to her."

"I thought it best not to tell her. She has no vice in her, but her tongue runs on, and she talks to everyone. I feel she may have inadvertently let out that I had that five hundred pounds in my office. I had that very day got it out in front of her to give her some money. She does not recall mentioning it to anyone, but cannot swear that she did not do so either."

"What time will she be going out?"

"Mr. Grindley is picking her up at three for a spin in his curricle."

"His curricle? But he sold it! He told me so himself, and Lord Harelson mentioned it as well. How did he recoup it? I begin to think I hit the nail on the head in fingering him. He could have bought a new curricle with Lady Harkness's money."

Dalton's face became pensive. "It bears looking into, but I would not publicly accuse him on no more evidence than a new curricle. He might have bought it on tick."

"He punts on tick, but what merchant would sell to him on credit when it is well known in town his pockets are to let?"

"There are always the moneylenders. He could be living on post-obits. He will come into his uncle's fortune one day."

"Really? I did not realize that."

"He is related to half the noble houses of England. It is his mama's brother, Mr. Greely, who will make him a rich man one day. Greely owns a shipping company."

"That explains why he is allowed into polite saloons in a borrowed shirt and spotted cravat."

"Now, you must not make the common error of judging a book by its cover, Miss Denver," he laughed. "Still, it would be interesting to know where Grindley was last evening."

"He was at Lady Verona's rout," I said, "but he left before us, I think, and had not showed up at Mrs. Lamont's when we left. In fact, Harelson said that he was to meet him there. He might have gone from the rout to Lady Harkness's house, then on to Mrs. Lamont's with his pockets jingling."

"He might have done," Dalton agreed, massaging his chin. "I expect he would know, in common with everyone else in the room, that Lady Harkness would not be going straight home."

"Was she at Mrs. Lamont's den? I am afraid I cannot remember what she looks like."

"The lady in black Chantilly lace."

"Oh yes, I recall her." One does not easily forget a lady decked out in black for a rout. She was a fading beauty who sought attention by bizarre outfits. "The constable ought to search Grindley's apartment."

"Officer Hutton will not be eager to come to cuffs with Harelson. I expect Harelson would take it very much amiss to have his house searched."

"It would only be Grindley's apartment."

"It ought to be done, but not, I think, officially. I shall mention it to Bow Street."

"By the time Bow Street arrives, Grindley will have gambled the thousand pounds away."

"Still, someone can keep an eye on the fellow in future. Shall we go to an insurance office now? I am nervous, knowing those fabulous pearls are not insured."

I was surprised and pleased that he meant to come with me. I got my bonnet at once, and he had his carriage brought around. "We could have sent for the agent to come to us," he said, "but it is a fine day for a drive, and the more often Miss Denver is seen about town, the better."

"I was seen about town all morning, with your sister."

"Linda mentioned bonnets and new gowns. I was

surprised you did not order new slippers," he quizzed. "I refer to your unaccountable habit of pitching perfectly good slippers out the window. I congratulate you on your aim. My missiles all missed their target."

"Were they keeping you awake, too, Mr. Dalton?"

He turned a flirtatious eye on me. "Something was, but I do not blame the cats entirely."

"Ah, you are referring to that other cat, named Tom."

"That, too." His manner implied I was the main distraction.

Miss Denver was seen driving the length of the Pavilion Parade before we stopped at the insurance agent's office at three. Mr. Milliken came back to Dalton's house with us after we were sure Lady Filmore had left. Dalton brought my jewelry to the saloon for examination. The agent made his examination with a loupe and a practiced eye that assured me Dalton had not yet pried out the stones. Like Dalton, he was more enamored of Lorene's pearls than the other gems. "That flush of pink—marvelous," he said. "And so perfectly matched. Wherever did you get them, Miss Denver?"

I told him the little I knew. "Wouldn't Tom like to get his hands on these beauties. Guard them well. I am insuring them for five thousand pounds."

The policy came to a shocking sum, but with a wily burglar on the loose, it was a necessary precaution. The agent enumerated the items and wrote up the policy; I wrote him a check, and Dalton showed him to the door. When he returned, he said, "Your carriage has just arrived, Miss Denver."

"My things from London! I must go home and oversee their placement. Thank you for your help, Mr. Dalton."

"Can I be of any assistance in your redecorating?"

"The servants will tend to it. It will be hard work, hauling furniture about."

"I have a strong back," he said, and followed me home.

When he removed his jacket, I was able to verify his proud boast. Those broad, square shoulders owed nothing to padding. There is something very attractive in a fine figure of a man without his jacket on. He looks more approachable, more familiar somehow. I was quite simply amazed to see Dalton pitch in with such good will. The furnishings of the saloon had to be pulled into the hallway to lay the Persian carpet over Lady Grieve's shabby floor covering. With Tumble on one corner, Dalton on one, and footmen on the other two, the carpet was laid in no time, and improved the room to some extent.

"Give the servants a glass of ale, Tumble," I said, when the job was done. "I can see to the placement of the pictures myself," I added aside to Dalton. "Would you like a glass of wine? Hauling furniture is hard work."

He lifted his jacket from the arm of a chair and tried to wiggle into it. It fit as closely as rind to a lemon. A sleeve became tangled, and I held it for him. I felt an unaccountable urge to run my hands over his back, but restrained myself.

"Thank you," he said, pulling his jacket down in front. "I would prefer ale. It is more refreshing when one is heated."

We both had an ale, and as I was eager to continue my redecorating, we removed the more lugubrious prints from the wall and hung my paintings. "I cannot imagine why Lady Grieve filled the house with second-rate pictures of the sea when she had only to peek out her window and she could see the real thing," I said, adjusting a nice landscape scene over the sofa. He lifted a black brow at me. I remembered the boring array of seascapes in his dining room, and felt rude. "In a saloon, I mean, where the sea is entirely visible from the window."

"Of course. The only spot for a seascape is in the dining room, where one has to walk six steps to see the real thing."

"Let us remove this dreadful clutter," I said, and began picking up statuettes and china dishes and other debris that littered every tabletop. "Fancy anyone paying money for such rubbish as this. Lady Grieve must have extremely poor taste."

"Auntie was never known for her taste in artistic matters," he replied blandly.

"Auntie! You mean Lady Grieve is your aunt, and you let me make fun of her all this time!"

"She is my mama's sister, but I like to feel I inherited my own superb taste from Papa. Except for the seascapes, of course. That, I fear, is a family failing."

"You are very sly, Mr. Dalton," I scolded, feeling a perfect fool.

"Let us hope I am sly enough to outwit Tom. As I have outwitted the canny Eve Denver, I feel success is within my grasp. Where do you want this box of rubbish put?"

He picked up the box of knickknacks, and I called Tumble to remove them. I went to the hall with Mr. Dalton. He picked up his hat and cane.

I said, "Be sure you don't tell your aunt what I said."

"It will be our little secret. I shall bring the pearls this evening. Will your aunt be accompanying us?"

"I don't know what her plans may be. Does it matter?"

"Not really. Linda will be along in any case." He looked a little self-conscious after this speech. It implied somehow that our behavior would be different, depending on whether we were alone or with others.

Of course, I did not reveal this intuition. "You did not tell me where we are going, Mr. Dalton."

"To a concert at the Theatre Royal. Signor Caravelli, the Italian tenor, is singing."

"Lovely," I said with so little enthusiasm that he smiled.

"I feel the same way. We can leave at intermission, if you wish, and find something more amusing to do." He put on his hat and left.

I busied myself arranging a few trinkets from home, and admiring the improvements in my saloon, and wondering what "more amusing" pursuits Mr. Dalton might have in mind.

Chapter Ten

I WAS UNSURE what degree of elegance was required for a concert at the Theatre Royal, but a string of pearls insured for five thousand pounds surely merited something approaching a grande toilette. With so little occasion to strut my evening finery in London, four gowns had proven sufficient. Until the nimble fingers of Madame Drouin enhanced my wardrobe, I had but little choice. Having already worn the pick of the crop, I was left with my indifferent blue crepe, featuring a narrow skirt and a maidenly bodice. This antique had come with me from Cornwall, where it was considered the latest jet of fashion a few years ago. The silver lace shawl would have helped, but after shivering to death at Lady Verona's rout, I did not plan to make that mistake again. I wore a white fringed affair, counting on the pearls to raise me out of the ordinary.

Hennie's comment, when I came down, was "You are never wearing that old thing, Eve!" You may imagine what this did for my self-confidence.

"Yes, I am. You decided to remain home, did you?" I retaliated. She was tarted up in her best gray gown, cheeks rouged to a fare-thee-well. She had already told me she was going to the same concert with Lord Brockley. That romance was certainly on the boil.

"I am going out with Lord Brockley," she reminded me. "If that is a dig at this gown, Eve, I call it downright shabby of you. I shall order a new gown tomorrow."

"Try Madame Drouin, on Paradise Street. Tell her I sent you. No argument, Hennie. You will put it on my bill." My temper breaks out at little provocation, but soon calms down.

"Maybe I will," she said, jiggling in discomfort.

"Order two gowns while you are about it. I ordered three."

"Three! Good gracious. David always said a penny saved is a penny earned. I had no idea Brighton would be so expensive."

"Or so much fun, eh, Hennie?" I laughed. We both shared a chuckle at our good fortune. I told her not to mention that I had left my jewels with Dalton, as Lady Filmore did not know.

"But I have already told Lord Brockley," she exclaimed. "You did not say it was a secret."

"Lord Brockley is not likely to steal them. Just ask him not to tell anyone."

"Why is it a secret, Eve?"

"Dalton feels his sister chatters too much. No point announcing to the world where my valuables are."

Lord Brockley called for Hennie shortly after that, inquiring in a hearty shout whether she was ready to hoist sail and be off. She nodded conspiratorially as she left, to let me know she would caution him to secrecy.

Dalton and Lady Filmore arrived shortly after. He was carrying the pearls in his pocket and handed them to me surreptitiously as he entered, so that his sister would not notice. There was not time to offer them a glass of wine, so I slipped the pearls around my neck while Lady Filmore fluffed at her curls at the hall mirror, and we were off to the Theatre Royal. Our seats were near the front. We had an excellent view of Signor Caravelli's tonsils, as he stood with his head back, hollering in

Italian. His singing reminded me for the world of the concert provided by the cats in the front yard last night.

Halfway through the first recital, Dalton leaned aside and whispered, "Could I borrow one of your slippers?"

"My aim is better."

"We'll leave at the first intermission."

A lady in front of us turned around and said, "Hush!" in a most impertinent way. We hushed, and had to satisfy our high taste by nonverbal grimaces after that.

"I had no idea an hour could be so long," Dalton said, when the first intermission finally came. "Let us go to the lobby and show off your necklace before we leave."

"The man sounds as if he were drowning. Such an artificial vibrato," Lady Filmore said.

"We'll leave before the torture resumes," Dalton said.

She accompanied us into the squeeze of the lobby but darted off as soon as we got there. I saw from the corner of my eye that she was chasing after Harelson. Poor girl. Someone ought to tip her the clue not to hound him so. Nothing was more likely to make him run for the hills. We met up with Hennie and Lord Brockley. That misguided gentleman praised Caravelli to the ceiling. Hennie, whom I can only assume had taken leave of either her hearing or her senses, seconded him in his praise.

Lady Filmore succeeded in catching Harelson, and they joined us, bringing wine with them, which was very welcome.

"A grand concert," Brockley said again.

"Very nice indeed," Harelson agreed.

"I think it is horrid. We are leaving before the second half," I announced.

Linda wore a scheming face. "Must we leave?" she said. "I would like to stay for the second half.

Harelson, will you give me a drive home?" So that was what she was up to. "You can take Richard's seat for the second half," she continued, not giving him time to think up an excuse. "It is much better than yours."

Harelson hadn't much choice but to agree. He did so with a good grace, like the gentleman he was.

"Where is Mr. Grindley this evening, Lord Harelson?" I asked, just out of idle curiosity.

"Out spending his money," he laughed. His eyes widened a little as they discovered my pearls. "He tells me he won at cards last night. A fool and his money are soon parted. He has already replaced his curricle and team, and will come home with his pockets to let tonight, if I know anything."

"That would be at Mrs. Lamont's that he won last night? You mentioned he was going there, I think."

"He did not show up, actually. He fell into a game with some chaps at the inn. He did not even know them; he was fortunate they were not Captain Sharps. I understand he is playing at the inn again this evening."

"With the same men?" I inquired, thinking Officer Hutton could check up on this.

"I believe he said last night's companions were traveling salesmen, and were moving on today. There is a sort of floating card game that goes on at the Rose and Thorn. That was his destination. I asked him to come here instead, but Grindley has no taste for music." His eyes returned once or twice to my pearls as we spoke, but he did not compliment me on them.

We talked for a few minutes, then some other people joined us, and Harelson and Lady Filmore went to join a younger set. When the bell for the second half of the concert rang, Dalton and I headed for the street door.

I said, "You heard what Harelson said about

Grindley? A pair of traveling salesmen make a good excuse for a sudden fortune. No one can check his story. He did not turn up at Mrs. Lamont's, where Harelson was expecting him."

"I can check whether he played cards at the inn."

"I am sure he did—using the money he stole from Lady Harkness as his stake. Did the man from Bow Street arrive, Mr. Dalton? This would be a good chance to check Grindley's rooms, while he and Harelson are both out."

"He will be arriving tomorrow morning."

"That may be too late. I daresay Harelson's house is full of servants, to make getting in impossible."

"No, he is roughing it. He makes do with his valet and one footman who doubles as butler, groom, and general factotum. They are free as soon as Harelson leaves for the evening. I happen to know his house is usually empty in the evening, as I have stopped by once or twice on Linda's behalf."

"Then this would be a good time to search it."

"I shall do that, as soon as I take you home."

"Why waste time driving to Marine Parade? Harelson's house is near here, is it not, on East Street?"

"I do not like to leave a lady alone in the carriage."

"Much better for me to accompany you inside," I agreed, knowing full well this was not his meaning. His weak smile acknowledged my remark as a joke, so I had to inform him that I was serious. "I am as much interested in catching Tom as anyone—more so, since I have been used as bait to trap him. Besides, there is no danger in it. You will knock at the door first to see if anyone is at home. Why, I would be safer inside with you than in the carriage."

"But safer still in your own home."

"Mr. Dalton, you have seen me 'under fire,' as the soldiers say, at Parker's pawnshop, and know that I am not one to lose her head. I think we both know I shall be accompanying you; let us not waste time in discussion. Now, how shall we get in if no one is at home? Perhaps the back door will be left ajar. It will be better to enter from the rear in any case, lest we are spotted by a chance passerby."

He drew a resigned sigh and said, "How are your skills at picking a lock?"

"I have had no occasion to practice lock picking. I was hoping for an unlocked window. We could use your carriage blanket to deaden the noise if we have to break it, but that would inform Grindley he has had an intruder."

"Leave your pearls behind. It has been my experience that something usually goes amiss in such a venture as this. The string might break, and it would be a pity to lose even one."

"I see! You are willing to risk my neck, but the pearls must not be put at peril!"

"Well, upon my word, if that is not just like a woman! You are the one who insisted on coming."

"I was joking, Mr. Dalton. Have you no sense of humor?"

"That joke had the sting of truth."

I removed the pearls and dropped them into the side pocket. Mr. Dalton pulled the check string and ordered John Groom to drive to East Street. We descended at the corner, and the groom drove along to park in the shadows beyond Harelson's house. The houses in this neighborhood were large and solid-looking, but not so elegant as those on Marine Parade. There was no traffic at this hour of the night.

"That is Harelson's house," he said, pointing to one much like its neighbors, except that no lights showed inside.

I hid behind a tree while Mr. Dalton knocked on the door. After no reply to his second knock, I joined him. "The front door is locked," he said in a low tone.

"We shall try the back."

The back was reached by a narrow, paved path. An arched gate led to the rear. There was a sense of abandon about the premises. Rank grass invaded the path, clutching at my skirt hem and no doubt marking it. Some dark hulks loomed up before us in the shadows, abandoned crates or rubbish bins or some such thing. Access was ridiculously easy. As I was pointing out an open window, Dalton turned the knob and said, "It's open."

We scuttled inside, closing the door behind us. A faint ray of moonlight at the window told us we were in the scullery. A teapot and the remains of a meal for two were still on the table. Harelson's valet and factotum, I assumed. I felt the pot; it was cold. We stood still for a moment, listening to the dead silence of an empty house.

"We shall need a light," I said, and began peering into the darkness. There was a lamp near the stove. Dalton lit it by sticking a straw into the dying embers of the stove and applying it to the wick.

We crept upstairs to the main floor. A ghostly saloon of adequate size, sparsely furnished, loomed on the left. We peered in and continued upstairs. "I wonder which rooms are Grindley's," I whispered.

Dalton spoke in a normal voice. "I shall recognize Harelson's things."

The first two chambers were obviously unoccupied. The beds were not made up, and the dresser tops were bare. The third door we tried was Grindley's. I knew instinctively that Lord Harelson was not so slovenly as to leave his dirty linen in a heap on the floor, and one boot on his bed. I lit another lamp, and while Dalton searched the clothes closet, I went to the desk. It was empty, save for a welter of bills (unpaid), and a receipt for fifty pounds, signed by Lord Harelson. That would be for Grindley's summer's rent. Not cheap either, for one room, but perhaps Grindley had the use of the saloon as well.

Next I went to the dresser, where a handsome leather-bound jewelry box held two pennies, a broken clasp knife, and a brass button from a man's jacket. There was a sound from below, muffled by distance, but certainly in the house, not outside.

"These old houses—squeaking rafters," he said vaguely.

I returned to work, quickly rifling the drawers, but found nothing incriminating.

"Nothing here," he said, turning from the clothespress.

"Perhaps under the mattress, or—"

We froze in place, as the sounds of footfalls coming up the stairs reached our ears. That "squeaking rafter" had been the front door opening. We knew Lord Harelson was at the concert, so it had to be Stewart Grindley, about to catch us red-handed searching his bedchamber.

I did not want to swoon in front of Dalton, after my proud boast of grace under pressure. As cool as cream cheese, I blew out the lamp and nipped over to the clothespress. "In here," I said, and climbed in, pushing Grindley's jackets aside.

Dalton grabbed the bedroom lamp from my hand and set it on the dresser, extinguished his own kitchen lamp, and wiggled in beside me, still holding the lamp. He drew the door to behind him. The smell of dying wick was powerful in that small, enclosed space. If Grindley had his wits about him, he would catch the same scent in the bedroom. I waited with my heart in my mouth for the door to open. What possible excuse could we give if we were discovered? Perhaps I trembled, or perhaps Mr. Dalton just wanted some physical comfort, or perhaps his arm was cramped in the confined space. In any case, he put his arm around my waist and pulled me more closely against him.

I tensed up like a coiled spring, but as I was prevented by circumstances from objecting either verbally or physically, I soon relaxed and enjoyed the unexpected intimacy. His breaths fanned the back of my neck, sending shivers down my spine. His fingers tightened their grip on my waist. I hardly dared think what liberty might come next—but whatever it was, I would have to submit to it in silence.

Chapter Eleven

THROUGH A CRACK in the clothespress door I could see that Grindley was carrying a lighted candle. He wore evening clothes, but still managed to look common. He sniffed the air a couple of times and looked around, but was apparently satisfied that there was nothing amiss. He strode purposefully toward the bed, lifted the mattress, and picked up something. Between the dim light and the small size of the article, I could not tell what it was, but I caught the wink of metal. He shook the object a moment in the palm of his hand, frowning, then slid it into his pocket and left.

We soon heard his footsteps running back downstairs, heard the front door close, and our hearts returned to our chests. I pushed open the closet door and stepped into a pitch-black room. I felt a little restraint from Dalton's arm, but that may be because I bolted forward unexpectedly. In any case, he did not try to detain me, nor did he turn flirtatious.

"Let us see what is under the mattress, then leave," I said at once. "This spree has killed my taste for adventure."

He relit his lamp, and we went to the bed. There was nothing under the mattress. We searched all the way around, and looked under the bed and under the pillow for good measure.

"I believe it was jewelry," I said, and described the metallic flash. "A ring, perhaps, or something small. It could have been an ear pendant. He has lost all his money at cards and is using jewelry for collateral."

Dalton rubbed his chin in a way I was coming to recognize was an habitual gesture. "That explains his hurry; he is eager to get back to the Rose and Thorn."

"You will be going there now?" He opened his lips, and I said, "Don't worry, I am not going to ask you to take me along. Should we have a look at the other rooms before leaving?"

"No, let us go before Harelson returns. Between bad singing and housebreaking, I have entertained you enough for one evening, but I shall let you know tomorrow if I learn anything at the inn."

When we returned below, the front door was actually hanging open. Grindley had been so eager to return to the card game that he had not bothered to close it properly. "No point bolting the door after the ring is gone," I said. We closed the door but did not try to lock it.

We slipped quietly out and went along the dark street to Dalton's carriage, parked in the shadows of a big elm tree. Dalton directed the groom to my house, and we were off.

"It looks as if Grindley is our man," I said.

"We have not proved anything, except that he is a shocking bad houseguest, leaving the door open. Thieves are usually more careful. Attention to detail is ingrained with them."

"Tonight he was not stealing. I daresay he is more careful when he is on the job, as it were."

"Hmmm. Before condemning the man, I should like to know what it was he removed from under the mattress."

"Why should he put anything beneath the mattress unless he wanted to hide it from Harelson? He would not have to hide his own jewelry, which suggests that whatever resided there was stolen.

His jewelry box was empty, incidentally. He has already hawked all his own valuables."

"Has he run through all of Lady Harkness's money so soon? A thousand pounds."

"He bought a curricle and team. That does not come cheap. The circumstances are all against him, Mr. Dalton."

"You, of all people, must realize the fallibility of circumstantial evidence, Miss Denver," he said, with a grin.

"Are you never going to forget the manner of our meeting?"

I moved my hand to the side pocket to recover my pearls, and felt cold steel. I lifted the thing out and found myself holding a pistol. For a joke, I poked it into Dalton's ribs and said, "You should have paid more attention to circumstances, Dalton. Stand and deliver."

I caught a fleeting glimpse of his face in a shaft of moonlight. To my shock and consternation, he had taken me seriously. His face was a mask of astonishment, tinged with anger. "You choose a bad moment, Miss Denver," he said, in a cold, hard voice. "I am not carrying much cash on me."

"I was *fooling*, Dalton! You cannot think—"

An uneasy laugh escaped his lips. "I knew that." But he was in a great hurry to recover his pistol all the same. He reached out at once and took it from me.

"Why do you have a pistol in your carriage? I hope it is not loaded."

"An unloaded gun is not much use. Best put it away before you accidentally shoot someone."

He put it in the other side pocket, while I retrieved my rope of pearls and placed them around my neck again. "Do you always carry a gun?"

"I only began to do so after Tom robbed me. I determined I would not be caught off guard again."

"I could have shot you easily," I crowed. "Why

did you not take it into Harelson's house? If Grindley had caught us, I would have been thankful for that pistol."

"That will teach me to go housebreaking with a lady. You were too much distraction for me," he replied, with a gallant little bow.

We were soon home. Dalton walked me to my front door. Nothing was said about his putting his arm around me in the clothespress. I was a little piqued about that, and more so that he had actually thought for even a moment that I was planning to hold him up with his own gun.

"Do I pass muster as an accomplice in crime, Mr. Dalton?" I asked saucily, to detain him a moment.

"No. I have just remembered another dereliction on my part. I left the kitchen lamp in Grindley's bedchamber. He will know, if he has his wits about him, that he had company."

"He will blame the servants."

"That chamber did not look to me as if it ever saw a servant from tip to toe of the week."

"True. It is difficult to comprehend a gentleman living in such a slovenly manner."

"Oh, we men are all savages beneath the skin. Prick any one of us, and you will find the primitive lurking."

"I do not think the savage is that close to the surface in you, Mr. Dalton."

"Don't count on it," he replied, with a suggestive smile. His tone, soft and low, spoke of romance. His hands rose and came slowly toward me, while his eyes glowed with admiration. His warm fingers touched my throat. The breath caught in my lungs, and just as I was about to close my eyes for a kiss, he removed the pearls from my neck.

"I shall return these to the vault," he said.

I felt warm all over from my folly. Had he seen my half-closed eyes, and the expression of a moonling on my waiting face? I said, "Yes, thank you, Mr. Dalton," in a stricken voice.

"I wish you will call me Richard. I feel like Papa when you call me Mr. Dalton. Now that we are partners in crime, it is time to lighten the formality, *n'est-ce pas*?"

It seemed, incredibly, that he continued blind to my behavior. "Very well, Richard, and you must call me Eve."

"I have been doing so all evening, beneath my breath. Good night, Eve." He placed a fleeting kiss on the corner of my jaw, and left.

I went into the house, pretty well pleased with myself and Richard. Hennie had not returned yet. It was just after eleven when I arrived. I had a glass of wine to settle my nerves, and thumbed through the journals. At eleven-thirty I decided I was hungry and asked Tumble for a sandwich. At twelve I had finished it, and still no sign of Hennie. The concert must have been over by eleven. What was keeping her? If Brockley had taken her to Mrs. Lamont's gambling den again, I would give her a good Bear Garden jaw.

At twelve-thirty my nerves were on edge, and they did not improve when Hennie came home, smiling like the village idiot.

"Still up, Eve?" she said.

"I could not hope to sleep while you were out with that gambler. I daresay you have been at Lamont's again?"

"No indeed. Lord Brockley took us all—Lady Filmore and Harelson and myself—to Cavendish Place for a late supper. It was lovely. Everyone was there."

Hennie left me with nothing to say except that I was disappointed to have missed it, which was true.

"Where did you and Mr. Dalton go?" she asked.

I hesitated a moment, then said, "We came

straight home. I had a sandwich while I was waiting for you."

She glanced disparagingly at the plate. "We had lovely lobster patties and a raised partridge pie. So rich, I could do no more than sample the Chantilly." She knew Chantilly was my favorite treat.

"Dear me, I wonder what David would say of such dissipation."

"Folks have to eat," she said airily. "What are you and Mr. Dalton doing tomorrow?"

"Nothing special."

"Tomorrow Timothy—he asked me to call him Timothy—is taking me to tea with Lady Collifer. She told me to invite you, too, Eve, but I told her very likely you would be in hands with your garden party for the next day."

Another treat denied me! As the garden party was my first party, however, I did plan to oversee its preparation personally. I wanted everything to be as fine as I could make it. My only retort was to say, "Richard mentioned dropping in tomorrow morning. He asked me to call him Richard."

"That is nice, dear." She smiled, unimpressed. "I am off to bed now. I would offer to give you a hand with the preparations in the morning, but Lady Filmore is taking me to Madame Drouin's to order those two new gowns you promised me."

How sharper than a serpent's tooth is an ungrateful aunt! I went to bed with a nagging headache, disliking to admit I was jealous of a fifty-year-old lady, but I was. Hennie was enjoying more social success than I, and more romantic success, too. Of course, I was happy for her, in a grudging sort of way, but it seemed to me a young man ought to pursue more urgently than an old crock like Brockley. Then I remembered Richard's arm holding me snugly against him in the clothespress, and that fleeting kiss on the jaw before he left, and had to content myself with that.

Chapter Twelve

I GOT A leg up on Hennie in the romance department the next day when Richard came calling with Lady Filmore. He brought me a bouquet of roses from his garden, and behaved altogether in a more suitorly fashion than before. The roses were compared to my complexion. How exceedingly trite it sounds, sitting there in black and white. I maintain, however, that when a handsome gentleman is handing a lady a bouquet of roses, she must be critical indeed to find fault with the accompanying speech. He also expressed admiration of my rather plain muslin gown.

"I thought we might take a spin toward Beachy Head in my curricle," he said. "Have a spot of lunch there, as Linda and Mrs. Henderson are busy."

It sounded lovely, but Beachy Head was twenty-five miles away. Even in a curricle, it would take two hours either way. Throw in lunch, and I would have no time to work on my party.

The ladies were in such a fever to get to Madame Drouin's that they left at once, chatting and laughing like schoolgirls. I concluded that Lady Filmore had also made headway with her beau last night.

"Is the Bow Street officer not arriving this morning?" I asked Dalton.

"I have already met with him. We had a good chat. He will be remaining in Brighton to assist the local constabulary."

"I am glad to hear it. You have not told me what

it was that Grindley took from his room last night, Richard. Was he at the Rose and Thorn as we thought?"

"Indeed he was. It was a ring that he used for betting. Nothing unusual, just a gentleman's ring with an onyx stone, and a small diamond set into it. I looked over the list of stolen items the Bow Street officer brought with him. The onyx ring was not amongst them."

"I daresay Tom has pulled off a few small jobs that were not reported. Was Grindley losing heavily?"

"Actually he came out ahead and bought his ring back. He spoke of it as being a memento of his papa."

"Why was he not wearing it?"

"Let us discuss it while we drive."

"I should enjoy a short drive, but I cannot go as far as Beachy Head. I shall be busy this afternoon. You have not forgotten my garden party tomorrow?"

We drove toward Beachy Head, but only as far as Rottingdean. It is a pretty little village. We got out to walk along the chalk cliffs, looking at the sea. The wind was brisk, and we went to the White Horse for tea to warm up after.

I was curious to learn how his sister was faring with her beau, and said, "Hennie tells me your sister is taking tea with Lady Collifer this afternoon. I expect Lord Harelson will accompany her?"

"I am not so sure of that. The romance seems to be cooling. The pity of it is that the less he calls, the more convinced she becomes that she is in love with him."

"That is so often the way. If she were the one to beg off a few times, perhaps his love would quicken."

"So I have told her, more than once. I dislike to see her trotting after him in public. That display last evening at the concert, for instance, was embarrassing. I am hoping she will improve, with your friendship. She will not learn any aggressive tricks from you, Eve."

"Are you referring to my still being single at twenty—in my twenties, sir? That is ungallant of you."

"Certainly not! Most ladies marry too young. Linda was hardly out of the schoolroom when she fell head over ears in love with Filmore. A lady of twenty-five would show better judgment." Dalton saw my quick flash of anger and was amused. "Your Foster is no model of discretion," he murmured.

"I have nothing to hide. Nor does my quarter of a century ensure wisdom. Aunt Hennie is close to fifty, and she is behaving like a greenhorn. What is your opinion of Lord Brockley, Richard? One tends to mistrust a sailor. I was nervous as a broody hen last night when she came home so late."

"You have been listening to rumors," he said. "There is nothing in that story."

"What story!" I exclaimed, coming to rigid attention.

"Why, the story that he had something to do with his wife's death. Those foolish rumors often surface when a man comes into so much money at a relative's death. Especially when the heir was alone with the invalid. Lady Brockley had been ailing for years. That she happened to die shortly after Brockley returned from sea was not a coincidence. He gave up his ship to be with her in her declining days."

"You mean the man is a murderer, and Hennie has been running around town alone with him? Good God!"

"I have just been telling you those rumors are untrue."

"That is as may be. Tell me the whole story."

"There is not much to tell. Brockley Hall is deep

in the countryside, isolated. Lady Brockley used to be sociable, but when she fell ill, she retired to Brockley Hall and had no visitors except a few local friends, and a doctor, of course."

"What ailed her?"

"I don't know, exactly. A sort of consumption, I believe."

"And she was very rich, you say?"

"She brought a considerable fortune to the match, but Brockley had the use of that while she was still alive, or could have, if he wanted. As he was usually at sea, he had nowhere to spend the blunt. It is a great injustice to tar him only because she died a month after he joined her."

"I must warn Hennie of these rumors."

"Is your aunt wealthy, then?"

"No," I admitted. "Her late husband had two livings, but there is not much money in that."

"Well then, unless Brockley takes to twirling his eyes at *you*, I think you worry for nothing. If that occurs, I promise you I shall take care of him."

That had an interesting proprietary ring to it, but it did not calm my fears for Hennie's safety. We soon finished our tea and returned to Brighton. At the door, Richard said, "I shall be in touch with you later about this evening. I have heard of no parties. Perhaps we shall enjoy a quiet evening at home, for a change."

This sounded promising, and I quickly agreed to it.

Hennie was back from the modiste when I got home. I only half listened to her raptures about her new gowns. She had left off gray, and ordered one in blue, one in mauve. I was eager to warn her about Brockley.

"I know all about that rumor. Brockley told me himself," she said grandly. "That is the sort of gentleman he is."

"Mighty generous of him, when he knew you were bound to hear it anyway."

"He knows I have two hundred pounds a year. He is not likely to murder me for that, when he owns an abbey, and has an income of ten thousand a year."

"That much!" I exclaimed, before I got a guard on my tongue. "I should bear it in mind all the same. Perhaps he has acquired a taste for murder, and enjoys it for its own sake."

She tossed her head angrily. I think I heard the word "jealous," but did not choose to challenge her.

I made a point to be in the saloon when Brockley called for her that afternoon. I looked daggers at the man, but found my nerve left me at the last moment, and did not either taunt him about his late wife, or utter any threats if he tried anything with Hennie.

After about two minutes of my glaring, he said, "Shall we lift anchor, Alma, while the fair wind holds?" It sounded odd. No one ever called Hennie Alma. Even David called her Hennie.

"Are you *sailing* to Lady Collifer's?" I inquired grimly.

As they went to the door, I overheard him say, "That young lady is cranky as a bag of cats. It comes from not having a husband, I daresay. That is no way to get one."

I did not hear Hennie's reply, which is as well for her, as it sounded supportive. It seemed the old tar was hatching a mutiny against me.

I called Cook to discuss the garden party refreshments. Tumble joined us to discuss the arrangement of tables. We decided to have a long table and chairs set up in the backyard, with food that did not require a deal of formal service. Not to be outdone by Brockley's dinner, I asked for lobster patties and a raised pie of game hen, along with hams and cold roast fowl and a good many side dishes. Tumble thought we needed more servants. He said he would arrange to hire extra footmen for the occasion. Cook would not permit any strangers in her kitchen. She would manage with our own female servants.

When all was settled, there was nothing more to do regarding the meal but hope for good weather. We could retire indoors in a pinch, of course, but what I really wanted was an alfresco party, to show the garden. I went out to speak to Luke. I wanted everything properly trimmed, with no dead flowers on the bushes, and no rough patches of lawn.

I had to admit that he was a capable gardener. The roses, especially, looked lovely. I checked the movement of the sun to determine where it would be around five, when I planned to serve the alfresco dinner. I did not want the guests sitting in the hot sunlight, yet I wanted them protected from the sea breeze by the yew hedge. It would be convenient if I could place the table not too far from the back door. I had found my spot and was about to tell Tumble when a voice called to me from the street. Glancing up, I saw two heads rising above the yews. Lord Harelson and his tenant had come to call.

"I warned you I would pop in one day," Harelson said, and lifted the gate latch to step into the garden. Grindley followed him. We exchanged lukewarm smiles, then I turned a warmer greeting to Lord Harelson.

"How nice to see you. I thought you would be at Lady Collifer's tea party. I was invited myself," I added quite unnecesarily, "but I was too busy to attend."

"I know it well. I was speaking to Dalton a moment ago."

"Ah, you were calling on Lady Filmore," I said, happy for her, and wondering why he had skipped Lady Collifer's tea.

"Met Dalton on the strut," Grindley said. "Is this

where you are having your garden party, Miss Denver?"

"Yes, in the garden," I replied, with a smile to Harelson.

"Where did you think Miss Denver would have it, Grindley?" Harelson joked.

"In her garden. Just said so. Where is your aunt today?"

"She is attending Lady Collifer's tea party," I told him.

"Dead bore. Wise to stay away. I say, Harelson—a tent. All the crack."

This curious statement left me quite at sea. Harelson explained. "I have a tent at home that Mama used to use for garden parties, but I think it would crowd this little garden, and hide your lovely flowers."

I had not determined the extent of his backyard during last night's visit. Presumably it was large, and had once been in a condition that his mama could invite guests into it without blushing. "I thought I would place the table here," I said, pointing out the spot.

"Excellent," Harelson said, looking all around.

"The awning" was Grindley's next attempt at conversation.

"There is a red and white awning to go with the tent," Harelson explained. "It might give a festive note to your little do. I would be happy to lend it to you, if you like."

"That sounds interesting. Is it difficult to put up?"

"Not at all. I shall send my groom off to fetch it. Grindley and I shall help the servants set it up." Grindley strolled off to smell the flowers.

"Has your friend lost all his money yet?" I asked.

"He still has his carriage, so I have some hopes he did not plunge too deeply last night."

He sent off for the awning, and while we awaited

its arrival, I asked if the gentlemen would like a glass of wine.

"Could we go indoors and be comfortable?" Grindley said.

"Certainly, if you prefer." I looked to Harelson, thinking he might reprimand his friend, but he just rose and offered me his arm, to lead me inside.

Chapter Thirteen

"YOU HAVE FIXED up old Lady Grieve's dungeon," Grindley said, glancing around at the saloon.

"I admire your improvements," Harelson said. He went to stand in front of a painting, studying it in the affected manner of a connoisseur, tilting his head this way and that, and murmuring about chiaroscuro, and composition. "Are you related to Lady Corning?" he asked, finally saying something I understood.

It was a painting of a lady he was studying so assiduously. It had no title; I had picked it up for an old song in the same secondhand shop where I had found the satinwood commode. The artist had signed the picture Kauffmann, so it could not be the artist he referred to. "You recognize the lady, Lord Harelson?" I parried.

"Lady Corning was much older when I knew her. I last saw this painting in her brother, Lord Hutching's, saloon some years ago. The place has been sold up now, I believe."

"I am no relation to the Cornings. I bought several pictures from an art dealer in London." This was not a complete lie. Surely a man who sells art is an art dealer, whatever else he may be. I noticed that Grindley was picking up objects from the table, and turning them over to read the names on the bottom.

Harelson said, "You have a sharp eye! I congratulate you. Angelica Kauffmann was a marvelous portrait artist. A pity she wasted so much of her talent on mythological works."

"Who the deuce is Angelica Kauffmann?" Grindley asked. For once, I appreciated his intrusion.

It turned out she was a famous artist from the last century who had contributed to the ornamentation of St. Paul's.

"What would the picture be worth?" Grindley inquired, again pleasing me.

Harelson suggested an inordinate sum. I swallowed my gasp of delight and nodded, as if confirming what I had paid. He went on to examine my other paintings. He was quite sure my picture of three shepherds was a Poussin but informed me sadly that the fat lady was only of the school of Rubens, and not actually from the master's hand. I had heard of Rubens, and I regretted that the one name I recognized should not be genuine. I boasted that I had more paintings in London. "I just brought a few of the lesser ones with me to lighten these dark walls."

"I hope you have taken precautions for the safety of your collection in London while you are away," Harelson said.

"I left some staff at home. You must pop in and see my collection when we return to London, as you appreciate art." I wondered if a dozen pictures quite constituted a collection.

"I should enjoy it. Thank you. Even these paintings you have here might be open to theft if you are not careful. I do not refer to a night out at the theater or whatnot, but if you should go back to London for a weekend, for instance, taking your servants with you, you might return to find empty walls."

"Are you referring to Tom, Lord Harelson?" I asked, keeping my eyes from slewing to Grindley. "I thought he only stole jewels and money."

"True," Grindley said.

"I was not talking about Tom," Harelson said. "I take it for granted you have taken precautions for your jewelry."

"Yes, I have."

"What sort of precaution?" Grindley asked bluntly.

"Careful precautions," I replied. As if I would tell him!

"Thing is," Grindley said, leaning closer, "if you have stuck 'em in Lady Grieve's safe—well, the whole town and its dog knows of that safe in the floor of the study."

"*I* do not know of it!" I exclaimed.

"She did not tell you! By Jove, what a strange old duck she is. Would you like me to show it to you?"

"I shall have a look later."

"So if your pretty baubles ain't in her safe, where are they?" he asked.

Harelson shook his head at the man's simplicity. "One would think to hear you that you were planning to steal them, Grindley." Then he turned to me. "There is not an atom of vice in Grindley. He merely retains the curiosity of a child."

"I will tell you where else they ain't safe, Miss Denver, is under your mattress," Grindley informed me. My eyes flew open at this speech. "I fancy Tom got right into my bedchamber last night." Harelson shook his head. "True," Grindley insisted. "Found the kitchen lamp on my dresser when I got home. Noticed the room was mussed up."

"How could you tell?" Harelson asked, with a smile. I could not acknowledge that I shared his amusement.

"Did Tom take anything, Mr. Grindley?" I asked.

"Nothing to take really, but he was there. Heard of my winning at cards."

Tumble came to tell us the awning had arrived.

"I shall show your servants how to set it up," Harelson offered.

"Help," Grindley said. This was not a call for assistance, but rather an offer to help Harelson.

I sent for two footmen, and we went out into the yard. "Do you want it in the back or front?" Harelson asked. "It attaches to the doorway. It might be in the servants' way when they are serving dinner. It has struts that stick into the ground."

"It would give a cheerful welcome at the front door, sort of set the mood. Let us put it at the front."

The awning was unfurled, displaying several spots of mildew, but overall it was a pretty thing.

"Need a ladder," Grindley said. "In the shed, daresay."

Luke went for the ladder. When the awning was unfurled and the ladder in place, I asked Luke to climb up and attach the hardware.

"Best let me do it," Grindley offered. "A bit of a dab at mechanical things."

I feared he would tumble off the ladder, but he surprised me. His awkward-looking body scrambled up it like a squirrel. At one point, he was even on the roof. He achieved the ascent from ladder to roof in one leap, with no difficulty at all. Almost, I am tempted to say, with an air of considerable expertise, such as Tom might possess. This, added to his curiosity about my jewelry, insured his place at the top of my list of suspects.

When the job was done, Harelson and Grindley left. I stood back and admired the awning, then darted into the study to find the safe concealed in the floor. I lifted a threadbare carpet at each corner, and found the safe behind the desk. A square of flooring had been cut out and a safe recessed into the floor, then the wooden plank put back in place. The safe door was not locked. I opened it, and found nothing but a few yellowing sheets of paper having to do with the purchase of the house.

I was just returning outdoors for another look at the awning when Brockley's carriage drew up and the two gray occupants got out. "Aha! I see you are flying the flag at full mast, Miss Denver," Brockley said, looking at the awning.

"Lord Harelson came by and suggested it. Do you like it?" This last was addressed to Hennie.

"It is mildewed" was her comment.

"Dandy!" Brockley declared, at which time Hennie decided it looked bright and cheerful.

He left Hennie at the door, but before leaving, he said, "I shall be in the nest, looking out for you around nineteen hours, ladies."

Richard had not mentioned the evening's entertainment. "What does he mean?" I asked Hennie.

"Nineteen hours means seven o'clock. The nest is the crow's nest."

"He said he will be looking out for us."

"We are all going to Timothy's this evening. He is having a little rout party."

"I hope you have not promised that I shall go."

"Oh, you are going. Linda was at Lady Collifer's tea party. She said she and Richard will take you. When we got talking, it turned out there was nothing on for this evening, so Timothy decided to have an informal evening, with a few friends."

I felt several nettle stings during this conversation. It was encroaching of Lady Filmore and her brother to assume I would accompany them, without asking me. Not that I meant to refuse, but to be told that you are going has a peremptory sound to it. And, of course, I had been looking forward to that quiet evening at home with Richard. I noticed, too, that Hennie had achieved a first-name basis with Lady Filmore before I had.

I gave her a withering look and said, "Will this be an informal party in the style of Lady Filmore's dinner party?"

"Oh no, much grander than that, I believe."

"It did not take you long to steal Lady Filmore's trick of understatement."

"That is better than stealing her beau," she said saucily. "Linda was very concerned that Harelson did not go to the tea party. She won't be happy to learn he was battened down for the afternoon with you."

"For God's sake, don't start spouting sailors' slang to me. You make yourself look ridiculous, Hennie."

"I don't know why you let the fellow hang around."

"You know my opinion of Lord Brockley. It seems there is no accounting for taste."

She shook her head at the mildewed awning and said, "Indeed there is not. Vinegar and water might bring it clean."

On this speech she went inside, and I went to ask Luke to see if he could clean up the awning with vinegar and water.

Richard sent over a note asking me if I was agreeable to attending Lord Brockley's party that evening. "We shall have our private party another time. I shall undertake to see you are not poisoned this evening, if you will agree to wear the stunning bronze gown you wore the first evening we met. Shall I bring the diamonds?"

I scribbled "Yes" on the bottom of his note and returned it. My spirits were completely restored to their usual height.

Chapter Fourteen

I OFFERED HENNIE a drive to the party with Richard and me, but her suitor's passion had reached such a pitch that he was coming to "take her aboard" half an hour before his guests arrived. She came to borrow a shawl to enhance her toilette until Madame Drouin finished her gowns. It was not necessary to borrow my rouge. Her cheeks told me clearly she had invested in a pot for herself.

We were both uncomfortable with our little quarrel, and made it up indirectly by chatting in a friendly manner of other things. I told her what Harelson had said about my paintings, and all my suspicions of Stewart Grindley. I did not tell her that I had entered Harelson's house the night before. The vicar's widow would disapprove, and she still reprised that role from time to time.

"Where, exactly, does Lord Brockley live?" I asked, just as she was leaving.

"Oh, did you not know? He lives in that beautiful big stone mansion at the corner of Grand Junction Road. I thought everyone in Brighton knew that. It is a famous landmark."

"Ah, that big old place near the fish market. I thought it was an abandoned building," I retaliated.

Our reconciliations did not last long these days since Hennie had set up as a flirt.

"It has magnificent gardens. About ten times the size of yours," she said, and flounced out, hugging my best paisley shawl around her ungrateful shoulders.

The first thing Linda mentioned when she and Richard called was the awning out front. I confessed at once that Harelson had supplied it, to get the matter out of the way.

"So that is where he was this afternoon," she snipped.

"He and Grindley stopped by for a minute."

"Did they have the awning with them?" she inquired boldly. Richard gave her an admonishing look, but did not say anything.

"No, they sent for it. Grindley and Luke put it up."

She chose to assume that Harelson had left at once, which was exactly what I hoped she would think. I rattled on with the story of Lady Grieve's safe in the study to be finished with the name of Harelson. I was not likely to reach a first-name basis with Lady Filmore at this rate. Next to landing Richard, my main summer's goal was to become her bosom bow. And, of course, to catch Tom. Richard did not find a moment to slip me my diamonds until we were in the carriage. I put them on while he distracted his sister with some bantering conversation.

Brockley's mansion was probably the finest house in town, after the prince's pavillion. It was austere outside, the better to rest one's eyes for the grandeur within. Gilt and red brocade and marble dazzled the eye at every glance. Hennie looked for the world like a housekeeper, in her old gray gown. I don't know what everyone must have thought of her catching Brockley's eye.

His informal party outdid even Lady Filmore's in number of guests and elegance. A regular battalion of footmen, all dressed in Brockley's beloved gray, scuttled about like mice, passing drinks. Lady Filmore's sulks vanished like dew in the morning sun when she spotted Harelson across the room. He smiled and nodded to us, and she was off after him like a hound on the scent of Reynard. I did not see Grindley.

Dinner was ridiculously formal, with a gray shadow of a footman hovering behind every chair, filling glasses before they were a quarter empty, and even pushing the cutlery closer to you as new courses were served. I was strongly tempted to tell mine to step back a few feet, but did not like to reveal my humble origins. There were numerous "Willing foe and sea room" toasts, in numerous wines as each new course appeared. At one point, there were not less than five glasses sitting on the table in front of me. I felt decadent. Imagine some poor servant having to wash all this crystal. How did Hennie, with her concern for the poor, settle this enormous waste with her conscience? "Waste not, want not" was one of David's favorite aphorisms.

After we left the table, the gentlemen settled in for more drinking, of port this time. I don't know where they put such a quantity of liquid. I felt as if I were awash. But they did not remain away so very long. When they joined the ladies, Brockley set a straight course to Hennie, who sat with me on the sofa.

"I saw you squinting your eyes at this outlandish house," he said to me. "It is a foolish place. My papa, you must know, was a friend of Prinny's and infected by the same bad taste. My abbey is nothing like this. I would redo this place in Bristol fashion, but it seems a shame to waste good money, when most folks seem to like it pretty well."

"It is magnificent, Lord Brockley," I replied. I did not say, or mean, that I actually liked such royal grandeur.

"It is well enough," he said smugly. "Would you care to have a peek at the gardens, my dear?" I assumed he spoke to Hennie, but he offered me his arm.

"Do come, Eve," she said. "I'll go with you."

As she would certainly go alone if I refused, I went with them. The evenings lingered long at this June season. It was not quite dark yet, but the failing sun robbed the blooms of their glory. Still, a garden at dusk is a pretty sight, and certainly Lord Brockley's garden was impressive. It stretched for several hundred yards. Somewhere in the distance a plume of water shot up from a fountain. An Oriental gazebo harked back to the prince's pavilion. Brockley mentioned that Nash had thrown it up for his papa, from Repton's design. The air was heavy with perfume. It induced a lethargy, or perhaps it was the heavy meal and oceans of wine that caused the feeling. I wanted to curl up on one of the benches and close my eyes.

It occurred to me that if this was how the charmed circle lived, my garden party would be outstanding for nothing but its simplicity. Perhaps I should suggest we play in the manner of the French aristocracy, and serve ourselves, dressed as shepherdesses. I had the bonnet for it.

Brockley and Hennie moved a little ahead of me, but as I could still keep an eye on them, I allowed them this much privacy. We were near the iron fence that protected the garden from the street. I glanced out and saw two bucks strutting along. One of them was Grindley, but it was at the other that I stared. I had seen that handsome face before. It had some significance for me, but I could not place it immediately. I had met so many new people the last few days. Suddenly it flashed into my mind where I had seen that particular face before. He was the man who had sold Parker the emerald ring at Shepherd's Market.

I pelted to the fence and called to Mr. Grindley, hoping to discover his friend's name. Grindley turned and waved, but kept walking. Brockley and Hennie heard my shout and joined me.

"Do you know who that man is, Lord Brockley?" I asked, pointing to the stranger.

"It looks like young Grindley," he said.

"No, no. I mean the other fellow."

Brockley peered out, frowning. "My eyes ain't what they used to be, but it looks like young Naismith. Do you know him?"

"No, I do not have his acquaintance."

"And you don't want it, though he is my own nevvie," he said, and immediately drew us away to admire the Nash-Repton pavilion. Some suitable words of praise issued from my lips from time to time, but my mind was elsewhere. Grindley and Brockley's nephew . . . and perhaps Lord Brockley as well, working in tandem?

I was keen to try this idea out on Richard, and went after him as soon as I could induce the lovebirds to leave the garden. I found him wandering the maze of corridors.

"Where did you disappear to?" he asked curtly. "I have been looking all over for you."

There was an open door behind us. I beckoned him into a room that resembled an Oriental bordello, or how I imagined an Oriental bordello might look. It had strange sofas of sinuous shapes, with only one arm, and feet that resembled a lion's paws. The usual amount of red and gilt were present, along with lamps imitating lotus blossoms, and an extremely ugly marble fountain in one corner. The water issued from the mouth of a dragon into a basin with real goldfish in it.

"Do you know a Mr. Naismith?" I asked, sinking onto one of the strange sofas.

"I know several of them. Which one do you refer to?"

"Brockley's nephew."

"Half the Naismiths are related to him. Naismith is his family name. It could be his brother George's sons, or his brother Alfred, or Leonard."

"Oh dear. The one I mean is tall, young, blond."

"They are mostly tall and blond. None of them favor Brockley in looks. Some think he is a changeling. Why are you interested in Naismith?"

"He is the man who hawked Lady Dormere's ring. He is a friend of Grindley. They were together in the street just now."

"Really! Now, that is interesting. I wonder how Naismith came to possess Lady Dormere's ring."

"Did you not see him, when you were waiting outside of Parker's shop in London, Richard?"

"No, I arrived only moments before you came out."

"Well, he must have some connection to Tom. Is it possible Tom is more than one man?" I told him my reasons for thinking so, emphasizing Grindley's nimbleness in scampering up the ladder and onto the roof.

"The others, perhaps, but not Brockley. He is too rich to bother. You have only to glance around you."

"What do you suppose it costs to have fifty footmen, one hovering behind each guest at dinner, pestering us?"

"No more than Brockley can afford."

"Who is to say he is doing it for the money? He obviously misses the excitement of life at sea. He cannot open his mouth without saying something about hoisting anchor, or clear sailing, or a willing foe and sea room. He cannot be as big a fool as he appears, if he was given command of a ship."

"More than one ship. He retired a rear admiral. I am not sure he was not a vice admiral."

"There you are then." I waited expectantly.

"What do you expect me to do about this?" he asked.

"We must have a look for some stolen jewelry."

"In this house?" he exclaimed. "It would take a week."

"He would not leave it in any of the public rooms. It would likely be in either his bedchamber, or his study."

"Very likely, but—"

"We shall begin with his bedroom," I said, and rose.

"No, really! We are guests in his house. We cannot—"

"We are not likely to be here as anything else, unless you care to call Bow Street. We may not have another chance."

Richard reluctantly followed me out into the hallway. People were roaming about, quite at random. When the hallway was empty, we scampered upstairs. Brockley followed the prince's, and no doubt his papa's, habit of having the entire house ablaze with lights. We hurried down the red-carpeted hallway, peering into rooms until we came to one done up sparsely, like a ship, with naval-looking clocks and barometers and things on the wall. They were round, encased in brass circles, and mounted on mahogany. The large portrait of Admiral Nelson over the desk pretty well settled that we were in the right room.

It would be an easy room to search. The furnishings were few, and simple. I closed the door and began rifling drawers and peering into closets. We had soon determined that the room was innocent, save for a leatherbound chest at the end of the bed. It was locked with a lock that defied tampering with. It would take a blacksmith a week to break that stout lock.

"This is hopeless," Richard said.

I agreed, and suggested we try the study. When we went below, Brockley spotted us coming downstairs. "Having a look about, are you?" he asked, in perfectly good humor. "Folks never can quite believe the quantity of rubbish my papa accumulated. I like things simple myself. They are striking up some music in the ballroom, if you youngsters would like to have a hop. Your aunt will be sitting down to cards, Miss Denver, if you want to speak to her about anything."

"Nothing, thank you," I said.

A footman had come into the hall and was standing guard. Further searching was impossible at that moment, so we escaped to the ballroom, where the musicians were playing a waltz. Richard swept me into his arms and we whirled about the floor.

"Now, isn't this more enjoyable than sneaking about like a pair of thieves?" Richard asked.

He was a graceful dancer, and I am no slouch myself in that department. Lorene liked to keep up with fashions as much as our isolation allowed. She had hired a caper merchant to teach us the waltz, so I could perform without blushing—at least for my dancing. I will not say that a few of Richard's comments did not raise a flush, for he was quite warm in his conversation that evening.

He regretted that Linda must so often accompany us on our outings. "I am beginning to wish she could win Harelson back," he said. "They were used to be well nigh inseparable in London last spring."

"I wonder what came between them."

"Another lady, very likely. He seems to like variety. He has been dangling after Miss Denver lately, I think?"

The hint of jealousy in his words pleased me. "Is your sister unhappy with me?"

"I cannot think why else she has taken to calling you 'that wretched woman,' when she used to like you very well."

"Oh dear! I most particularly wished to make her my friend. I hope she does not think I am encouraging Harelson."

"I think you could *dis*courage him, if you felt so

inclined. A little of the vinegar you showed me in the park last week might do it. I am referring to your veiled threats when you asked me to empty my pockets."

"I have no reason to mistrust Harelson. I cannot be rude to him, or ask him to empty his pockets."

"You suspect everyone else of being Tom. Why not Harelson? And don't say because he is a nobleman. You suspect Brockley."

"Harelson did not murder his wife."

"Neither did Brockley. But I should not disparage Harelson with no real reason. I accuse him of nothing more than dangling after an heiress."

"Surely he has money of his own!" I exclaimed in surprise.

"He is comfortably off. His elder brother gets the estate. I notice his flirts usually have money."

"I understand your sister has no fortune."

"Precisely. Harelson was not aware of that when he took up with her. She thought he loved her for herself. I daresay one of his friends tipped him the clue."

"If that is the case, she is well rid of him."

"Yes, and so are you, Eve," he said, gazing into my eyes. The bit of Atlantic trapped there was stormy.

It was a pity that Harelson joined us at the end of the dance and asked me to stand up with him. It seemed impolite to refuse, but I claimed a great thirst. When he offered to take me for wine, my invention failed. I went with him, but I asked Richard and Lady Filmore to join us. Richard refused; she tagged along, of course.

There was one thing I hoped to learn from Harelson, and after he had procured us a glass of wine, I said, "As Grindley is a good friend of yours, Lord Harelson—"

"I wish you would call me Harelson. All my friends do."

I smiled uneasily at Lady Filmore and continued. "Do you happen to know which of the Naismith boys Grindley chums around with?"

"He goes about here and there with half a dozen of them."

"Do you know which of them he was seeing this evening?"

"He said nothing to me, but I know Robert is in town, for I saw him today. Very likely it is Robert. If it had been George or Tony, Brockley would have invited them to his do. He does not much care for Robert."

"Oh really. What is wrong with him?"

"A scapegrace lad. Gambling, and so on. Why do you ask?"

"No reason," I said, foolishly. "I saw Grindley with a fellow. Brockley thought it was a Naismith. He sounded rather peeved. I was curious; that's all."

"If Brockley was in the boughs, then we can assume it was Robert." I now had a name for Richard to give Bow Street.

I turned my next conversation to Lady Filmore. After five minutes of intensive flattery, she asked me to call her Linda, and I asked her to call me Eve. While all was rosy, I slipped away and left her alone with Harelson.

Richard was at the door of the ballroom, timing my absence. "I could not refuse a drink, when I had just said I was dying of thirst," I explained, before he could chide me.

"It is not my place to tell a grown lady what she may or may not do. The footmen have left the hallway. Shall we give the study a try?"

I took it for a favor, as I was morally certain he did not wish to do anything of the sort. Before we discovered the study, however, a footman discovered us and asked if he could help us, so we said we were looking for the card room, and he directed us there. Richard suggested we have a hand with Hennie and Brockley, and that is how we wasted the remainder of the evening. I would have preferred to dance, but with Harelson on the prowl, I settled for cards, and won three guineas. Brockley had no skill for whist at all. Even Hennie, who is a bit of a dab at the game, could not keep him from losing.

At midnight, Richard went to look for Linda to go home. She said Harelson would see her home, and we left, alone together.

Chapter Fifteen

A FOG AS thick as Tewkesbury mustard had rolled in while we partied at Brockley's place. It was so dense, you could hardly see a foot in front of you. It was strange driving home, like driving through clouds. The clip-clop of oncoming horses and rumble of wheels would be heard half a minute before the lights of an advancing carriage appeared. Unlike the famous fogs of London, this was a gentle, white mist, sweet-smelling, untouched by the smoke from factories. It was a warm evening, too, which made the fog seen friendly. I asked Richard to open the windows and let the mist in.

We drove up to see Prinny's pavilion in the fog. It looked like a fairy castle or a dream, with the domes and minarets glowing mistily through clouds—the very attar of romance. Then we drove directly home. I was sorry we had so short a distance to go, and even sorrier I had to destroy the mood by business.

I told Richard it was Robert Naismith who had been with Grindley. "Brockley pretended to dislike him, but he would not admit in public that he was friendly with such a sad creature."

"Let us forget about catching Tom this evening," Richard said. His hand fumbled in the darkness and seized mine.

"Do you have a more interesting topic for conversation?" I inquired discreetly.

"Now that we are alone, for once . . ." He lifted

my hand. I felt the brush of his lips pressing on it. It caused the strangest sensation within me, as if warm little fingers were exploring my vitals.

When he drew me into his arms, the warm fingers rose to my lungs and squeezed them fiercely, robbing me of breath. Soon his lips were seeking mine. "Richard!" I gasped, for I felt a maidenly show of reluctance was called for. The gentle roughness of his cheek grazed intimately against mine. The mist caused our faces to cling together.

"Hush, woman," he said softly, and his lips crushed mine.

The compelling intensity of the experience caught me off guard. The first mellowing pleasure swelled to a surge of excitement, crashing and thundering in my ears, as wild and elemental as the stormy sea at Cornwall. The heat of his embrace escalated to a pounding assault on my senses, and left me witless, but a willing prey to his fierce attack.

People may say what they like about the moon and starlight, about the romance of a garden or an apple orchard; for a really soul-destroying kiss, there is nothing like a carriage on a foggy night. It is as though you two were isolated in some imaginary land, surrounded by a beneficent, moistly soft, concealing Nature. As if you were in the clouds.

Soon—too soon—the carriage drew to a stop, and Richard reluctantly withdrew his arms. He sent the groom on and walked me to the door, with his arm around my waist, our hips bumping familiarly. I wished I could think of something light and clever to say, but as this situation was entirely new to me, no such comment came to mind.

"Isn't it a lovely night," I said stupidly.

"An enchanting night," he replied. He had no more idea what to say than I had myself.

We just looked at each other and laughed conspiratorially. I said, "I expect you will relieve me of my diamonds, before I go in."

"The ball is over, Miss Cinderella." He held out his hand.

"Then I had best scamper away, before you see me in rags." I removed the necklace, and a shimmering cascade of diamonds fell into his outstretched palm.

The cats were at it again that night. They chose that moment to begin their racket. "Is your glass slipper handy?" Richard asked.

"I wonder whose cats they are."

He made no reply to this, except with his eyes, which studied me engrossingly. "You look very lovely tonight, Eve," he said, in a husky voice.

"You have seen me in this gown before. It must be the fog that dims your view."

"That must be it," he agreed, with a quizzing smile that belied the words. If that was not the smile of a lover, then I had no right to be called a rational person.

I gave him the key; we walked to the door, opened it, and I went inside. When I reached to recover the key, he leaned down and placed a fleeting kiss on my lips, as light and evanescent as the touch of a butterfly.

"You look good in lamplight, too. I shall leave, before you raise the lights and frighten me with your warts and wrinkles."

"A wise precaution. Good night. I had a lovely time."

"A demain."

He turned and walked off into the fog. I went upstairs immediately, in a fog of my own. Strangely, the cats did not bother me that night. They made a frightful racket, but I was able to ignore it. My thoughts were all happy ones. Richard had been charming. After reliving every instant of that fateful drive home, I turned my thoughts to my garden party. I hoped the fog was not a harbinger of bad weather on the morrow.

I only stuck my nose out the door once in the morning, to check the weather. The sun was shining in the halfhearted way it usually shines on the coast, dulled by that perpetual layer of moisture, but with no indication of a storm approaching. I was busy with the servants and Cook. There was some little uncertainty whether we had sufficient glasses and china. Lady Grieve's house came fully furnished, but furnished with her second-best stuff. Her better things would be in London, or at her country estate. I wished I had brought some of my own superior tableware with me. Lorene had left me a silver table service for twenty-four.

When Linda came over to see if we required anything, I arranged to borrow two dozen wineglasses from her. She did not remain long, as she could see I was busy, but before she left, I asked how it had gone with Harelson last night.

"He left soon after you and Richard. Brockley and Mrs. Henderson brought me home. Did your aunt not tell you?"

"I was in bed when she got home last night, and I have hardly seen her this morning. She went to Madame Drouin's. One of her gowns is ready for the party this afternoon."

"Well, Harelson did not even drive me home," she said crossly, and left.

Tumble had been behaving himself well since coming to Brighton. I had put him in charge of buying wine for the party. He would know what the ton preferred. From the size of the bill he handed me, I assumed he had done me proud. I soon realized he had been sampling rather heavily. It was Hennie who informed me of this disaster when she returned.

"Tumble is weaving about the front hall like a reed in the wind, Eve. He was scarcely able to open the door. You must get him out of the way before the guests arrive."

"Good God! I counted on Tumble to oversee the serving of dinner. He knows better than my servants how to do things."

When I rushed out to see how bad he was, he fell over in a heap, wearing a beatific smile, and smelling like a winery.

It took two footmen to get him to bed. I searched his room myself, and found three bottles of a very expensive claret under the mattress. I removed them and locked his door, praying that he would be sobered up in time to greet the guests at four. That was the way the whole day went. Sauces turned thin or lumpy in the pan, cakes fell as flat as pancakes when they were removed from the oven, and the stove began belching smoke.

It was really the outside of enough when Hennie, who had not lifted a finger to help all day, came to complain that Madame Drouin had made her gown a little snug around the waist.

"Very likely you have put on weight since having it measured," I snapped. "God knows the only exercise you have had is walking from the table to Lord Brockley's carriage. Go without lunch. That might help."

She took me at my word, and refused to come to the table. By three-thirty some semblance of order had been achieved. Cook got a gallon or so of coffee into Tumble and assured me he had shaved and was nearly sober, but very cross. I found, to my consternation, that my new gown from Madame Drouin was also a trifle snug. I had not put on an ounce of weight, and could only conclude that the great Madame Drouin had no notion of fitting a gown. I would certainly take both it and Hennie's gown back for alterations at Madame's expense. My gown looked well, however. With my leghorn bonnet in place, I felt Richard might not find me repulsive, even without benefit of the fog.

At a quarter to four I strolled out into the garden

to see how things were shaping up, and uttered a howl of dismay. The table looked fine, the weather held up, but the garden was entirely stripped of blooms. What on earth had happened to the flowers? I rushed about from corner to corner, staring at a plentiful supply of leaves, but no blooms. I dashed to the rose garden. It told the story. Freshly cut stems stood out on every plant. That *fiend* of a Luke had purposely cut the flowers. I soon figured out why. He was selling them to some shop in Brighton, as he had the berries.

I spotted him moving about in the doorway of the garden shed and stalked toward him, hands clenched, steam issuing from my nostrils. "What have you done to my garden?" I demanded.

He gave me a witless, frightened smile. "I trimmed it up fresh first thing this morning, miss, for your party." He had the audacity to lift the shears, to show me what he had used.

I grabbed them from his hands. "Liar! You cut every single bloom, and sold it in Brighton. Don't bother to deny it, you brass-faced thief. I have a good mind to cut off your hand." My voice echoed shrilly in the small wooden shed. I opened the shears and snapped them shut, to frighten him.

He snatched his hand away as if I really meant to sever it from his arm. He cowered against the back of the shed. "Oh no, miss! I only trimmed the dead heads."

"Get out of here, you lying, thieving villain. Get out of this house, and never show your face here again. I shall notify Lady Grieve what you have done. And don't expect to receive your salary either. I have a good mind to call the constable and have you thrown in jail."

Luke looked over my shoulder with terror in his eyes. "She's gone mad!" he said, and ducked out past me. I turned to castigate him some more, and saw Richard's shocked face staring at me. His eyes flew to the shears, then he looked to Luke's fleeing back. He looked as frightened as Luke.

"Have I arrived too early?" he asked, in a hollow voice. "I came to see if I could help, but I see you are managing on your own."

It was the last straw, to be caught at the height of my shrewish behavior by Richard. Things could not possibly get any worse. I knew I was going to either strike him in frustration, or cry. I threw myself on his chest and bawled. "He has *ruined* my garden. Everything is going wrong. Tumble is drunk, and the cake fell, and my gown is too tight."

He removed the shears from my hand and set them on the shelf, then drew me to a bench in a sequestered corner, where there used to be pretty pink and white flowers, with tall purplish ones behind. It was now a desolate waste. I just pointed to it and hiccuped a sob.

"That whelp ought to be whipped," he said angrily. I drew a sigh of relief. Good! He was blaming Luke, and not me.

"I know perfectly well he cut them and sold them. It is not the first time either," I said. "He stole the berries I promised Linda, and he sold them. My servant had to buy my own berries to give you. I recognized the boxes."

His lips moved unsteadily. "There was no need to buy us berries. You should have told me what happened. It is a pity he decimated your garden, Eve, but it is not really the flowers folks are coming to see. It is you. You don't want them to see you like this."

He took out his handkerchief and dabbed at my eyes and cheeks. "It is not just the flowers, Richard. Tumble was drunk as a skunk this morning. He is sobering up now, but he is still cranky, and I have no doubt he will be foxed before an hour is up. I counted on him to keep an eye on things."

"You should never count on Tumble," he said.

"He has let down every hostess who ever hired him. I shall send my butler over to give you a hand."

"Would you?"

"Consider it done. My Ruthven is a wizard. Now, what else disturbs you? You mentioned your gown—it looks charming."

"It is not so *very* tight. If I don't eat anything, I daresay it won't split."

"Your bonnet is fetching," he said, flicking a finger against the broad brim.

"Thank you." I smiled wanly.

He squeezed my fingers. "Is everything going to be all right now?" I nodded. "I expect it was just a case of last-minute fidgets. Linda is the same before a party. I keep the butcher knife well out of her way. I shall go and fetch Ruthven. Go and wash your face. Your guests will be here soon."

"Thank you, Richard," I said humbly. I felt a perfect fool, but much better. Especially I was grateful that my awful temper had not disgusted him. He had been very sweet. "I am not usually so horrid," I said apologetically.

"Don't apologize, my dear. It is best for us to know each other in all our moods before—ah, here is Brockley."

"You greet him," I said, and nipped into the house to bathe my eyes, and tell Hennie her beau had arrived.

Chapter Sixteen

I AM HAPPY to report the party was a success. Ruthven orchestrated the serving of refreshments and tended to a few minor catastrophes, such as Mrs. Jenkins tripping and spilling a glass of punch down the front of her gown. He did the whole smoothly and with such good humor, he quite put Tumble in the shade. The guests exchanged sly looks, to see Richard's butler taking orders from me. It seemed to suggest a more complete blending of our households in the future. Lady Collifer whispered in my ear it was "plain as the town pump I had nabbed myself a parti." I blushed to my ears and stoutly denied anything of the sort.

"There are no secrets, living in such a gazebo as Brighton." She smiled.

If anyone noticed the lack of flowers, they were too kind to say so. I mentioned Luke's trick to a few people, who just shook their heads and smiled. "Is that not always the way," they would say offhandedly, and rush on to something else.

Brockley said, "Aye, but he is a fine gardener after all. You must take the crust with the crumb. You are flower enough for us, Miss Denver." Pleased with his compliment, he repeated it to Hennie ten minutes later.

I must concede that Linda, in her new bonnet, took the prize for beauty, but I grant myself second place. She was in smiles that day as Harelson was attentive. I did overhear them arguing once, down by the shorn rose bushes. "You *gave* it to me," she said, in a hurt tone.

"Things are different now, Linda."

"I have not changed my feelings. Have you?" she asked.

"Of course not."

"Well then."

Grindley ambled along at that moment. "Jolly fine party, Miss Denver. See the awning is holding up."

"You did a good job, Mr. Grindley. I saw you last night, over the fence of Lord Brockley's place. I don't believe I recognized the gentleman with you. You should have brought him along today."

"Naismith," he said.

"Which Naismith? I understand there are several of them."

"Clive."

"Ah." Robert, I said to myself. Why was he lying?

"Couldn't have come anyhow—Naismith. Back to Eastbourne—flat races today."

"And what did you do last night?"

He scratched his ear. "Had a few wets with Naismith. How was Brockley's do?"

I took this quick question for an attempt to distract me, but did not pursue the subject further. I had not heard of any robberies by Tom last night. "It was a very nice party."

"Place gives me the megrims. Too red, and too rich for my taste. But then, Brockley measures his blunt in bushels. Ah, there is Ruthven. A glass of wine, if you please. I am dry as a lime basket."

I circulated among my guests, receiving compliments and polite smiles. I have no idea where Tumble spent the afternoon. Hennie told me he had taken a pet when Ruthven was brought in over his head, but I did not care for that. I meant to be rid of Tumble as soon as I could find a replacement. A gentleman might be able to handle a drunken butler; a lady would be a fool to attempt it.

I had thought my party would break up about seven. The last stragglers did not leave till eight o'clock. With no outing planned for that evening, I hoped Richard and I might finally have that quiet evening at home. Brockley and Richard were the only two remaining.

"Let us go in and have a cup of tea," Hennie suggested.

I hoped our quiet evening would not end up a game of whist with her and Brockley.

"I am promised to the pavilion for cards," Brockley said. "Prinny landed in this afternoon and had his press gang shanghai a crew of us into service. Het or wet, snow or blow, he will have his game of cards. Difficult to refuse."

"Of course, you must go, Timothy." Hennie tossed a proud peep at me, as if to say, "See how high my beau flies."

He left, and the three of us went inside for tea. "Should we invite Linda over?" I said to Richard.

"She mentioned attending the play with Lady Collifer. I daresay Harelson will be of the party."

"There is nothing like a nice cup of tea, after the turmoil of a party," Hennie said. "It went pretty well after all, Eve. You worried too much about Luke cutting the flowers."

I looked sheepishly to Richard. "It was my nerves."

Ruthven, who was overseeing the cleanup operation, came to the door with a note for me. "It came by special delivery on the coach from London, madam," he said.

I tore it open and found myself looking at Polke's crabbed letters. "The house was broke into lass nite while I was visiting my fambly in Cheapside, Miss Denver. All the silver is gon, plus the dark old picshure of the man in the nightcap that was hanging over the new chest in the saloon. Should I call in Bow Street at all?"

"I have been robbed!" I gasped. Richard grabbed the note. Hennie jumped up to read over his shoulder.

"All the silver stolen!" she howled. "Lorene's good silver. Full table settings for twenty-four. I wonder if the serving dishes are gone as well."

"That idiot, Polke, had not even the wits to call in Bow Street. I must go to London at once, Richard."

"There is no point setting out in the middle of the night. We shall leave early in the morning and be there by noon hour."

"Mercy, I must send a note off to Timothy," Hennie said, and went to the study.

"I shan't sleep a wink. I think I should go tonight," I said. "Ironic that my London house should be robbed, after scheming to lure Tom into robbing me in Brighton. This was not the work of Tom, of course. He takes only money and jewelry."

After a frowning pause, Richard said, "He might take other valuables, if he had time and privacy in an empty house. I don't rule Tom out. He knows you are safely in Brighton."

"Grindley!" I exclaimed. "He had no real account to give of his whereabouts last night. And he lied about Naismith, too."

"What do you mean?"

"He said it was Clive Naismith he was with. I have reason to believe it was that scoundrel Robert."

"But if Grindley and Naismith were here in Brighton . . ." He examined the note again. "Polke doesn't say at what hour the house was robbed. Did he stay the night with his family, I wonder, and only discover the robbery in the morning?"

"I must get home and ask him these things."

Richard reached out and placed his hand on my

wrist. "Let me think a moment," he said. I waited, and he began murmuring to himself. "It could be a ruse to get you back to London, to give Tom easy picking of this house."

"Grindley was asking pointed questions about where I keep my jewelry. I did not tell him, of course. I think you are right. He is trying to get me out, so he can rob this house."

"It looks that way. But then, he would not expect you to take your servants."

"All the world knows my butler is a drunkard. The other servants would be asleep on the top floor at three or four in the morning. I wager the sly rogue is skulking in the shadows this minute, waiting to see if I leave. What should we do?"

A sly smile curved his lips. "We shall oblige him."

"I don't understand."

"We shall leave, head for London, and sneak back, to catch him red-handed. We may not have another chance like this. We may be mistaken, but it is worth a try. What do you say?"

After a very brief consideration, I said, "I can be ready in five minutes."

"No hurry. Tom has no way of knowing you have received that note from Brighton. Although he would know the evening coach does bring special delivery messages from London. As you did not mention the theft at your party, he might have been on the qui vive to see if a messenger from the London coach came here. I am assuming Tom is either one of our friends, or has access to them."

"I do not consider Grindley a good friend by any means, but somehow or other, he always shows up every place, including my own party. When shall we leave?"

"Let us give it, say, an hour, to make sure Tom gets his message." I noticed he avoided using Grindley's name.

"Brockley has got himself an ironclad alibi. He is playing cards with Prinny at the pavilion tonight," I mentioned.

He gave me a disparaging look. "Do you think your aunt is also involved, Eve?"

"No, I think she is being duped entirely by the old tar."

I refilled our teacups. "This is not the sort of quiet evening I had in mind when we spoke of it earlier," Richard said, which at least showed me he regretted missing that treat.

"There will be plenty of evenings."

He looked at me askance, causing me to fear I had assumed too much. But when he spoke, it was not of that. "I have something to confess," he said, rather humbly. "It was not Linda who inserted that advertisement announcing your departure for Brighton. I did it myself, for the purpose of informing the world, and Tom, that you would be here. That was my plan, to use you for bait, from the minute you mentioned coming to Brighton. I didn't know you then. . . . I put you into this dreadful house for that sole reason. I never intended for you to actually be robbed, of course, but this is my fault nevertheless, and I shall replace whatever has been stolen."

Other than telling me it was he and not Linda who had inserted the advertisement, the only new twist here was that word "sole." He had implied earlier that he found me attractive, that he wished to have me living next door for my own sake.

"That is not news to me. I suspected as much all along," I said, feigning indifference.

"I am truly sorry, Eve."

"If I am Tom's victim, I have no one to blame but myself. I started this whole thing by taking Lady Dormere's ring."

We sipped tea for a while in silence, both thinking our own thoughts. "I shall change into a more comfortable gown before we leave. I wonder what is keeping Hennie. We shall take her with us, of course. Tom will be more likely to break in if none of the family is at home."

"I don't like to subject an older lady to such a tiring night. We will have to walk back to your house from some distance, so that Tom does not see our carriage. Perhaps she would prefer to spend the night at my house. I'll ask her, while you change."

It was a relief to get out of that tight gown. I chose an older, dark gown—older in case it got soiled, and dark for concealment in the shadows. Of course, Richard's admission that he had not immediately been smitten with my beauty rankled, but I felt confident things had changed since then. He had not been acting last night in the fog. I regretted the loss of Lorene's silver, but I had high hopes of recovering it. Overall, this Brighton visit had been a wonderfully exciting adventure. I did not regret it a bit, even if I never saw the silver again.

Hennie came bustling into my room as I tidied my hair. "I am going to spend the night at Dalton's, Eve," she said. "I don't relish a dart to London in the middle of the night if you don't need me. I added a line on the bottom of my note to Timothy, in case he comes."

Brockley was by no means off my list of suspects. "Have you sent the note yet?" I asked.

"Dalton is taking care of it for me."

I nipped smartly downstairs. "About that note, Richard. Do you think we should send it?"

"Why not? In the unlikely case that Brockley is involved, he won't let Mrs. Henderson's presence next door stop him. In fact, it implies we trust him."

"That's true. She believes we are really going to London. I did not tell her the difference."

He nodded. “We’ll take my carriage. My team are faster.”

“And you have a gun.”

“Let us hope it does not come to that.”

Chapter Seventeen

BOTH BACK AND front doors of Lady Grieve's house were much in use during the next hour. We wanted Tom, if he was watching, to see that some commotion was going forth to alert him that we had received the note, and were preparing to flee to London. Ruthven went out by the front door to summon the carriage. Richard accompanied Hennie to his house, and brought back his own overnight case. All this activity was to distract Tom from observing the back door, where a footman was dispatched for the Bow Street officer, and where the officer appeared in person thirty minutes later, wearing the livery of Richard's footmen. Did I mention it was a dark bottle green livery, very handsome?

"Frank Ketchen, of Bow Street, Miss Denver," he said, and shook my hand. "I borrowed this disguise to fool Tom."

As he spoke, he darted to the window and closed the curtains. Next he checked to see that all the doors were secure. He was a little gray slug of a man with thinning gray hair and brown circles around his sunken eyes. That "slug" referred to his complexion; in movement he was like a fly, darting hither and thither. He looked as if you could blow him over with a flip of your fan, but he carried a gun, and assured me he could shoot the eye out of a pigeon at a hundred paces.

He was to be on guard indoors in case Tom came

before we returned. Richard's watchman patrolled the grounds each night.

I asked Ketchen if he required anything to assist his vigil. "Coffee. Strong, black, and lots of it," he said. "I would be obliged if you'd tell your servants they are to take orders from me, in case of an incident."

I called Ruthven and gave the order for him to relay. I also ordered Ketchen's coffee. Ruthven suggested a flask for Richard and me to take with us. He was that thoughtful sort of butler. At last Ketchen sat down, but not to rest. He drew out a notebook and took a description of my silverware. I could only describe the flatware, as I did not know what else had been taken. "Oh, and one painting," I added. "Not valuable."

"Subject of said picture?"

"An old man. Just his head," I replied, and described the gilt frame in more detail.

"Occupants of house?"

"Jimmie Polke, footman."

He even asked to see Polke's note and inquired whether the scribbling was Polke's. "I am not an expert. It certainly looks like his writing. It is written on my stationery."

"Any criminal record? You'd be surprised how many robberies are done by servants."

"He has been with my family for fifteen years without stealing so much as a teaspoon."

"That you know about," he murmured under his breath, and jotted down "No known criminal record" beside Polke's name.

The sixty minutes between our decision to leave and our actual leaving seemed more like six hours, but at last the carriage was waiting. I snatched up a closed pitcher of coffee and my bonnet and we were off.

I was surprised to see Richard's traveling carriage and a team of four, when we were only driving a mile out of town. I said, "Would your curricle not be faster and less bother?"

"We would not drive a curricle all the way to London at night. We do not want Tom to suspect our trick. Let him see we are setting off on a journey."

"I had been looking forward to a ride in the open carriage," I complained, but got into the lumbering coach and had to settle for an open window.

Richard was in a feverish state of excitement, as I was myself. "This might be the break we have been waiting for," he said, smiling softly to himself. "You will be a heroine, Eve."

"All I did was get myself robbed. You are the hero, sir. It was your idea to have Tom rob me, and also your idea to make this mock trip to London to entrap him."

He smiled modestly. "I set my mind to it that I wanted to catch Tom, not only because he robbed me, but because he sets a bad example. He gives young men the idea they can steal with impunity, making a laughingstock of the law. Since Bow Street seemed powerless to catch him, I decided to give it a go. Mind you, Ketchen will want his share of the glory. It will mean a promotion for him, I should think. Some of the stolen gems carry a reward on their heads."

"We should give the money to charity, Richard. There are so many people less fortunate than we."

"I would like to do something for homeless children. Education is the magic key to lift them out of a life of misery and eventually crime."

That was the sort of noble mood we were in, feeling we were a couple of heroes, out to save the world. We drove north for a mile through the dark night, peering out the window at frequent intervals to see we were not being followed. It was a suitable night for danger and intrigue. A fingernail of moon and a sprinkling of infinitesimally small stars looked lost in the enormity of the black heavens above. They did little to illuminate the countryside. A wind soughed through the trees by the border of the road. It sounded human—a sigh, or a moan.

Before we had quite decided whether to establish an orphanage or a good day school with the reward money, we came to the crossroad that had been settled as a good place to turn the carriage around. The horses slowed nearly to a halt. As we were halfway into our trip, I decided to take advantage of the slow pace to pour us a cup of coffee.

"My groom is going to drive in here and back the team out, since the road is too narrow to make a turn," Richard explained. The team slowly made the turn.

"It is a very narrow side road, and with a ditch on either side. If you had driven your curricle—"

"John Groom can turn this rig on a penny," he replied complacently. The team began to back up.

The next sound was a wild whinnying from the team, and a shout of "Whoa! Steady, lads!" from John Groom, as the carriage leaned precariously into the ditch.

"I daresay John Groom cannot see that penny in the dark," I said.

Richard stuck his head out the window and hollered, "Pull ahead and try again."

The nags moved forward, and we slowly eased out of the ditch. "Why do you not continue along this road until you come to a farm, and turn in the normal way?" I suggested.

"I don't see a farm up ahead. There are no lights."

"Farmers would be in bed at this hour. There must be a farm, or why would there be a road?"

"It would take too long." Again the jingle of the harness and shuffle of hooves indicated that the horses were being backed up, although the carriage did not immediately move.

"The horses are frightened. Give them a touch of the whip," Richard called out the window.

There was a gentle crack from the whip, and the team moved more quickly, pushing the carriage right into the ditch this time. It did a half turn in the air, throwing me against the door. Richard tumbled down on top of me, cursing a blue streak.

"You're hurting my arm!" I shouted, trying to extract it from beneath his shoulder.

He tried to get up, but had difficulty as my door was acting as the floor of the carriage, and there was very little foot room. John Groom came to our aid. The other carriage door was in the roof position, looking up at the sky. The groom heaved the door open and gave Richard a hand out.

"How are the nags?" was Richard's first concern. Never mind that I was lying in a painful heap on the floor.

"I stopped them before they followed the cart into the ditch. They're right as rain."

"We'll see if we can tilt the carriage upright and have them pull it out," Richard said.

"Would someone mind pulling me out!" I shouted crossly.

Richard reached down and gave my sore arm a yank. I howled. "Careful! You nearly broke my arm when you fell on it."

I reached up with my good arm, knocking over the pitcher of coffee, spilling the entire contents into my lap. And it was quite hot, too. "Help! I'm scalded!"

Richard gave a mighty heave, and I came sailing up through the door in the ceiling, dripping with hot coffee, and cursing almost as proficiently as Richard had done. "For God's sake, watch what you are about! Between my broken arm and my dislocated shoulder from that yank and scalding coffee—"

"Sorry." He reached out and daubed at my sodden gown. "It doesn't feel so very hot," he said apologetically.

"Well, it is, and furthermore, both arms hurt like Hades."

Richard swooped me up in his arm and handed me down to John Groom, who was standing on the ground. "Put her over there," Richard said, as if I were a sack of grain. He tossed his head toward a clump of trees, to indicate my resting place. He had at least the courtesy to accompany me, and take off his jacket to form a bed on what felt like a patch of nettles.

As soon as he determined that I was not in actual danger of expiring, he and John Groom went to tend to the carriage. I just sat, watching. My fuming anger turned to amusement as they struggled. First they tried to do it by sheer manpower. After a deal of grunting and heaving, they unhooked the team to get a better grasp at the carriage. When this effort failed, they unsuccessfully endeavored to harness up the team in some new manner that gave them greater "leverage." There was a deal of talk of "leverage." Nothing worked. That carriage was there to stay until a team of stout bullocks came to rescue it.

Eventually I became bored with the show, and decided to be well again. I put on Richard's coat, as the wind on my wet gown made me chilly, and joined them.

"I daresay Tom has come and gone by now," I said. I do believe Richard had forgotten all about him. There is something about a gentleman's horses and carriage that take precedence over everything else. "If you had taken the curricle as I suggested . . . I wager it really could turn on a penny."

"The team could have done it. It is the demmed dark that caused the problem."

"Did you think the sun would be shining at midnight?"

"It is only ten-thirty."

"We have been gone at least an hour. Let us hope Ketchen is more effectual than—" He turned an icy stare on me. His face looked like an angry gargoyle, carved in stone.

"You are only a mile from town," John Groom said. "You could hoof it back, and send help from Brighton. I'll stay with the rig."

Richard thought about that for a moment. "Are you able to walk, or would you rather sit in the carriage?" he asked me.

"I don't usually walk on my hands. There is nothing wrong with my legs. The sooner I see a doctor, the better. I can hardly sit in a carriage when the seats are at right angles to the floor. I believe there is some law to that effect—the Law of Gravity, I believe they call it."

"What you might do," the groom suggested, "is stop at the first inn and ask them to send help."

Richard nodded. "Take good care of my cattle. There is a pitcher of coffee in—"

"On my gown, actually," I reminded him, and turned to walk down the road alone.

Richard caught up with me after a moment. The first hundred or so paces were taken in utter silence, as we mentally nursed our grievances. I cradled my right elbow in my left hand. The elbow was not broken, but it truly was sore.

"How is the arm?" he asked, in a suitably apologetic tone.

"The doctor will know whether it is broken."

"I am sorry, Eve. Here, I'll make a sling from my cravat."

"That is not necessary."

He insisted on doing it. He yanked off his cravat and tied a great white strip of muslin around my neck, gently inserting my arm in it. "There, that will hold you till we can get you to a sawbones."

"Careful, Richard. If you hurt any other part of

my anatomy, you will be stark naked by the time we get home. I have already got your jacket and cravat."

"Serves me right. It is all my fault. I should have brought the curricle."

"Or at least driven forward until you found a proper place to turn around."

"Did the coffee burn you very badly?"

"The blisters won't show. They are on my—torso," I said vaguely.

He looked at me in alarm. "Are you sure you should be walking? I could run ahead to the inn—"

"And leave me here alone? The way our luck is running, I would be set upon by Black Bart." Bart was the most infamous highwayman that year.

We trudged on a little farther. "I wish I had worn walking shoes. I feel every pebble in these thin-soled slippers."

"I fear my Hessians would be too large. Would you prefer to walk through the fields?"

"No. Thank you."

After another little silence he said, rather sheepishly, "I daresay we will look back on this one day and laugh."

"I daresay. I wonder what I will find more hilarious: rolling in the ditch, your appalling language, or being dumped under the tree like a sack of potatoes."

Richard gave over trying to lure me back into a good humor and said bluntly that in future he would be wary of lemons wearing the rind of sweet oranges. I was obliged to retaliate that I would be on the alert for Greeks bearing gifts of real estate.

Eventually we came to an elegant inn that catered to the gentry. "Thank God it is a decent place," he said, as we approached the door. The hostler in the yard gave us a very squinty look.

The patrons in the lobby did more than squint.

They said quite audibly to the clerk, "I thought this was a decent inn!"

The uppity little clerk treated us like the commoners we resembled. "You are in the wrong place, folks. The Pig and Whistle down the road caters to your sort."

It was difficult to maintain any countenance when I caught our reflection in a mirror: me in my old, stained gown with the brim of my bonnet mashed out of shape, and Richard sans jacket and cravat, with his hair all tousled about. His boots were dust-laden, and his shirt covered with grease from the carriage. Even our faces were dirty.

Richard assumed his angry gargoyle expression and said, "Shut your face or I'll remove your teeth. I want to hire a rig to take us to Brighton."

"We don't hire out dog carts," the uppity clerk said, tossing his nose in the air.

Richard drew his purse out of his pocket and emptied a wad of bills on the counter. A scattering of gold coins clattered noisily after. Then he reached across the counter and lifted the clerk up by his shoulder pads until his feet dangled in the air. "Are you familiar with the name Black Bart?" he growled, glaring into the man's frightened eyes. The clerk swallowed a couple of times and nodded his head. "Then you'll have a story to tell your kiddies, if you're man enough to sire any kids, and if you live that long. I'm Black Bart, and you're going to get me a rig from your stable. *Now!*"

This speech emptied the lobby faster than if he had shouted, "The Black Plague!" Customers flew in all directions.

The clerk reached out and hit a bell that rested on the counter. Richard let go of his jacket, and the man fell to the floor with a thump. A page boy darted forward in response to the bell.

"This gentleman would like a rig to go to Brighton," the clerk said, in a strangled voice. "Right away." Behind Richard's back, I saw him mouth the words "Black Bart!" The page boy goggled in delight. It is really a shame that these youngsters make heroes of common criminals.

"And a team to draw my carriage out of the ditch," Richard said. "You'll find it half a mile north." He picked up a gold coin and flipped it at the page boy, who snatched it out of the air and disappeared, grinning from cheek to cheek.

"How much do I owe you?" Richard asked the clerk.

"No charge, sir. A pleasure to serve you, sir."

Richard shoved a bill of an inordinately large denomination at him and took me by the arm to leave. "He'll have a constable after us, Ri—Bart," I warned.

Richard turned back to the clerk. "You wouldn't be fool enough to go doing that, lad?"

"No, sir. No, sir!" I think he crossed his heart, but perhaps he was just clutching at it. Certainly he looked as if he might have a stroke at any moment.

"Good lad." Richard grinned menacingly, and we left.

"Did you ever consider a life on the stage, Richard?" I asked in a weak voice when we were out the door.

"It was easier than trying to convince him we're respectable."

"Yes. It makes one realize clothes do make the man. Perhaps we should spend the reward money on new jackets for the poor children. Except that there will probably be no reward."

He drew out his watch. "It is only a quarter past eleven. We might still catch Tom."

The hostler brought forth a spanking whiskey drawn by a pony.

"I paid enough for a proper carriage!" Richard objected.

"Never mind, Bart. It is good enough."

He assisted me into the whiskey, hopped into the driver's seat himself, and we were off. "He did not believe you were Black Bart, or he would have provided a better rig," I said. "He probably thought you were just a dangerous lunatic."

"I wonder what he thought of you," Richard retaliated.

Chapter Eighteen

WE REACHED BRIGHTON without incident. As we could not drive up to the house in the whiskey, Richard left it a block away and we walked via the back road to my house. At some point during our absence, Ketchen had had all the lights put out, which made good sense. Tom would not try to enter until everyone was in bed. We crept from bush to bush through the garden without encountering Richard's watchman. It seemed impossible it was only hours ago I had entertained society here. Now all was dark and quiet.

When we reached the house, our trials continued. The back door was locked, and we disliked to make any racket, in case Tom was waiting in the shadows, or in the house itself.

"How can we get in?" I whispered. "I did not bring my key with me."

"I wonder if Aunt Grieve's key is still on the ledge over the door." He reached up and, amazingly, found it.

"You should have told me it was there! Anyone might have found it."

"No one did, so there is no harm done," he said blandly.

He slid the key into the lock and opened the door. With so little moonlight, the kitchen looked like a cave, save for the glimmer of pots hanging on the wall. We crept along quietly, heading for the stairs that would take us up to the house proper. Richard's elbow bumped against a bowl on the table and sent it flying. It was Cook's bread, set out to rise. The wad of dough flew out and hit me in the face. It felt like a huge, soft hand. I stifled a scream and pulled it off. It was nothing short of a miracle that the bowl landed silently in a basket of laundry.

We reached the door, and Richard pushed it open. He took just one step into the darkness beyond, before he was felled by a stunning blow. All I could see was a shadow moving above him, then he disappeared.

Naturally I assumed Tom had got in, had heard us, and struck Richard down. I stepped back, feeling around for a weapon. You would think in a kitchen equipped with all manner of cleavers and knives, one could come up with a better weapon than a teapot. In the darkness, and in my haste and fear, however, it was the teapot that my fingers encountered, and it was the teapot that I raised to go after Tom. I swung blindly into the doorway, and connected forcefully with a head. A hollow one, to judge by the echoing sound.

A grunting noise was heard, not from my victim, but from the floor, where Richard lay. Concerned though I was to see whether he was alive or dead, instinct led me to ensure my own life first. I swung again. A strong hand reached out and seized my arm. The teapot fell with a clatter.

"I arrest you in the name of the law," Ketchen declared.

"For God's sake, Ketchen, let me go," I said, and wrenched my wrist free. "If you have killed Richard . . ." I flew to him, just as he rose up from the floor, shaking his head. "It's all right, Richard. It is only Ketchen," I said.

Richard struggled to his feet. "If I die of a fractured skull, I will die happy, knowing I was killed by Bow Street."

"Let us have some light," I declared.

Ketchen carried a dark lantern. He allowed us one quick peek to see there were no impediments in our way. We stepped around the teapot and the puddle oozing from it, found the stairs, and mounted to the saloon.

"There's only one room where we may safely have a light," he told us. "That wee bit of a parlor off the dining room."

I said brusquely, "I don't know about you, Richard, but I am ready to forget Tom for tonight, and light the saloon."

"Now you see an officer's duty is not all cracking heads and chasing murderers and shooting thieves. There is a deal of work to it as well," Ketchen informed us. "After waiting here for two hours, *I* am much of a mind to sit it out and have done with Tom Cat once and for all."

With this lure to sustain us, we went to the wee bit of a parlor off the dining room and allowed ourselves the luxury of a lamp. "My eyes tell me you have had a tumble," Ketchen remarked, when the light revealed our condition.

I adjusted my arm sling, which had come loose. "It is reassuring to know Bow Street is awake on all suits, Mr. Ketchen. We have been bruised to the backbone and marrow."

He gave Richard a wire-drawn smile in appreciation of my temper. Richard suggested I would be better off in bed, while he and Ketchen stood guard, but I elected to remain below. There followed a few of the most stultifyingly boring hours ever endured by humankind. First we listened, and we occasionally imagined we heard a sound outside, but it invariably came to naught. No private conversation was possible with Ketchen playing propriety between us. The talk was all of Tom. Ketchen asked for a description of the picture Tom had stolen from my London house, and I described it.

"It was a portrayal of an old man's head. I believe he had a cravat at his neck, although he was not wearing a jacket."

Something in my description caught Richard's interest. "Was he wearing a hat?" he asked.

"He had something on his head. It blended into the shadows behind, so it was difficult to tell."

"You say you bought it from the same shop where you bought Lord Hutching's commode?"

"That is right. I bought several pieces there."

"Good lord!" he said weakly. "The missing Rembrandt."

My ears perked up at this stupendous statement. "Missing Rembrandt? Don't tell me I have been robbed of a Rembrandt!"

"Old Lord Hutching certainly had a self-portrait of the artist, similar to the one you have described. When he died, his brother from Ireland inherited the estate. He was a wastrel, who sold off the silverplate and paintings bit by bit, to finance his dissipation. He mortgaged the house, and eventually lost it. The Rembrandt disappeared from view. What did you pay for the painting?"

"A crown—for the frame."

Richard's face fell in astonishment. When he had recovered, he rose and said grimly, "We are wasting our time. The London theft was no ruse to get you out of your house, Eve. Some art thief learned you had the Rembrandt, and went after it. It has nothing to do with Tom."

"Ketchen, you must recover it!" I exclaimed.

Ketchen shook his head wearily. "I daresay all of London and his brother knew you had the thing."

"No, none of my callers ever mentioned its being a Rembrandt. It was in a dark corner, you know. You did not notice it when you called, Richard?"

"When I realized the painting in the entrance hall was an inferior imitation of Van Dyke, I assumed your other paintings were of the same sort."

I thinned my nostrils at this description of the portrait in my front hall, hung there as I considered it the best of my "collection."

Ketchen, listening, spoke up. "What of the plate that was taken? Your art thief will not usually take the family silver."

"It was in a safe in my bedchamber," I told him.

"At Bow Street, we find they nip in, take what is worth taking from the walls, and get out quick as winking."

"I shall go to London and see what else is missing."

"I'll know the whole by morning," Ketchen said. "I fired off a note to Bow Street to look into it before coming here. If your Jimmie Polke was away all night, then the thief had ample time to rummage."

"And Brockley, or any of his guests, had ample time to get to London after his party," I countered. "I'll wager he only had that party to give himself an alibi."

Ketchen said, "I'll stake my head 'twas a London rogue. They make merry as soon as the gentry trot out of London at the Season's end."

"Then we are wasting our time, sitting here in the dark," I declared, and strode into the saloon, where I lit every lamp in the room, and removed my sling to pour us a glass of wine.

"The least morsel or bit of the grape rushes straight to my head," Ketchen admitted, "but as I am off duty, I shall join you." He accepted his glass with enthusiasm. "Watching and waiting is thirsty work."

The wine, added to the lateness of the hour and the day's many exertions, made me drowsy. After a couple of yawns, Richard said good night and took his leave. Ketchen said he would just stretch out on the sofa, if I had no objection, and remain till morning, just in case.

"You are perfectly welcome to stay, Mr. Ketchen. I shall get you a pillow and blanket."

When I returned, he had refilled his glass. The grape was going to his head. He was more relaxed, and freer of tongue.

"Townshend puts great faith in Mr. Dalton," he said.

"Yes. Tom relieved Mr. Dalton of some money, so naturally he is eager to help Bow Street."

"So I have heard. Townshend shares all his secrets with Mr. Dalton. Dalton had seen your Rembrandt . . ."

"He had seen it, but did not recognize it."

"So he says. And he knew of the safe in your bedroom?"

"Yes, but I trust you are not suggesting that he is the thief! You have had quite enough wine, Mr. Ketchen." I took the bottle with me when I left.

It was utter nonsense to think Richard had anything to do with any of these thefts. He had given a perfectly reasonable explanation of why he had been loitering outside Parker's shop the day I met him. Yet if he had been surreptitiously keeping an eye on his accomplice, Robert Naismith, it would explain his eagerness to leave when the constable appeared. It was odd, too, that I had never once spotted the watchman he claimed to have guarding my house. But then, how to explain his returning Lady Dormere's ring? She had written on her own stationery to thank me for it.

He was rich as could be. Why would he steal? I remembered Linda claiming that Richard had become such a skint. He used to be more generous. I thought of my jewels, stored in his safe. He had ample time to have them copied. He usually suggested which jewels I should wear. Was that to prevent my choosing a piece he had given a jeweler to have copied?

Surely I was not being conned by a clever gentleman? Surely he was truly fond of me. Or my fortune . . . This could not be true! Why had we spent an extremely trying evening in a mock flight to London, if Richard knew perfectly well no one was going to break into my house? It would all make more sense in the morning, I decided, and finally went to sleep, just as the rosy fingers of dawn lightened the sky.

Chapter Nineteen

HENNIE WAS ALL bright-eyed and bushy-tailed and full of gossip when I joined her for breakfast the next morning. Although my sore arm had recovered, my few hours of worrying in the dark left me limp and crotchety. As sleep proved elusive, I rose early and was downstairs at my usual eight o'clock. Ketchen had left.

"No luck in catching Tom?" Hennie inquired, with a smirk.

"No. I expect Richard told you he failed to come." I gave an account of our fruitless night.

"Richard was still in bed when I left. Your servants are in a rare pelter this morning, Eve. Cook says the bread she had set out to rise was on the floor; the teapot minus its spout was in the hallway, with tea running all over. She is threatening to report Ketchen to his superior."

"I shall speak to her later. What on earth is that thing you are eating, Hennie?"

"Biscuits, since the bread could not be baked. Luke is back in the garden with his tail between his legs."

"I told him he was not to return."

"Timothy says he really is a wonderful gardener, if you could only stop him from selling everything he grows. Now that the season is begun, folks have hired up all the local labor. People like you, favored above the norm by God, should show compassion to the less fortunate."

"Must you quote both husband and lover to me in one speech, Hennie?"

"Timothy is not my lover! You make it sound like a cheap smack-and-cuddle affair. It is nothing of the sort."

"Sorry. I suppose I shall give Luke another chance."

Cook brought a nice big bowl of strawberries. "From Luke," she said, with an appealing eye. "Mary is sweet on him. She says if he goes, she goes." Mary was my favorite servant. "He is ever so sorry, Miss Denver. It is just that he has always had the excess produce, you see, as part of his wages."

"He has an odd idea of 'excess.' " I meant to keep him, but I would let him simmer a little longer. "How was your evening, Hennie?" I asked, to let Cook know we were finished with discussing Luke. Cook gave me a jaundiced look and left.

"Harelson brought Linda home early. She was very upset."

"More trouble with him?"

"He is not good enough for her, but she is eager to get a home of her own. Richard *seems* nice, but she says he is always scolding her for her expensive habits."

It was obvious to anyone who knows her that Hennie wished me to join in her disparagement of Richard. She gets a certain gleam in her eye. "I don't blame Richard. Linda spends like a drunken sailor."

Hennie bridled up at this slur on her lover's profession. "All sailors are not drunken wastrels. Timothy never overindulges. He is a simple man."

"I noticed. But we were discussing Linda. She is only sore because she cannot land Harelson. If he does not come to the sticking point, she should go after someone else."

"He did propose last spring; that is the odd thing.

He even gave her an engagement ring, but in secret, not to be worn in public. She had slipped it on last night. Harelson and she were alone when I went over, you know. I would not have noticed the ring if he had not kept squinting at it. Then Linda became flustered and took it off and put it in her pocket. Harelson seemed angry when he left."

"What excuse does he give for not wanting her to wear it?"

"He told Linda it is a family heirloom. People might recognize it and suspect they are engaged. It is quite distinctive. A star sapphire done in what she calls a cabochon cut, round and smooth, like a small blue cherry, set in gold prongs. He wants her to give it back, though he swears he is still mad for her. She holds on to it because it is all that keeps him calling."

"He does not act like a man in love. What is the great secret in their betrothal? Richard would not object, I think."

"Harelson told her a cock-and-bull story about his papa wanting him to marry some lady back home. He will be cut off without a sou if he disobeys, and all that sort of claptrap. There is no saying Richard will do anything for Linda if she marries a penniless man. He has had his fill of them with Filmore. She was in tears, Eve. She asked me not to mention the ring, so you must not say anything to Richard."

"I wish you had not told me. I dislike this duplicity."

"Try the berries," she said, endeavoring to lure me into a good mood. "Cook has supplied this clotted cream to go with them. Sprinkle a little of this castor sugar on the berries." I ate the berries and cream and biscuit without tasting them.

"I promised Linda I would look in on her after breakfast," Hennie said. "Will you come with me, Eve?"

"You go ahead. I must mollify Cook, and speak to Luke."

"We might go out for a drive later, to cheer her up," Hennie said, then she got her bonnet and went next door.

I sallied forth to wage domesticity. First I called Cook and apologized myself back into her good graces. Then I sent for Luke, and after severe admonitions, agreed to give him another chance.

"The thing is," he said, "Lady Grieve always let me have the excess produce."

"I am aware of that, Luke. What salary did she pay you?"

I learned that she paid him exactly half what I was paying him. "If you would prefer to return to your old salary and have the excess produce, we will settle for that," I said. He took the extra cash, and I, in a benevolent mood, said he might have any produce we did not require for home consumption.

When all my unpleasant duties were taken care of, I still felt unsettled. Those seeds of doubt Ketchen had planted last night began to sprout. I should be on my way to London to recover my silver and my Rembrandt, but I was loath to leave.

Richard, I felt, would offer to come with me, but those seeds of doubt grew apace. I could not quite believe Richard was Tom, but if he was only courting me for my fortune, I must be rid of him. And all the friends and social activity he had brought would leave along with him.

Surely Richard was not the notorious Tom. There were more likely suspects. Grindley, Naismith, Brockley. Even Harelson might be involved. If he loved Linda and would lose his fortune if he married her, he might take to a life of crime to finance marriage to the expensive wench. My mind wandered back to a snatch of conversation overheard at my garden party. What Harelson had been asking Linda to give him back was the ring.

At nine-thirty Hennie returned, bursting with news. "Linda is going to visit Lady Grieve, in London. She had a letter, and said she most go at once. I asked if her aunt was ill. She said no. Then she said yes, then she told the servants to pack a bag, as she would be leaving on the ten-o'clock coach. Richard was still in bed. She said he might want the carriage himself."

"It is unlike her to be so thoughtful. I really should go to London myself to see what all is missing. Hennie, would you mind running over and offering her a seat in my rig?"

"Will you want me to go to London with you, Eve? You will not want to be alone in the house, with only Polke."

"I expect you have plans to see Brockley?"

"I had a note from him this morning. When the prince is in Brighton, he has no time for me," she said, with a sniff.

Hennie went to speak to Linda. She was back in five minutes. "I just missed her. Ruthven said he had called a hansom cab for her. I saw one flying down the street as I crossed the yard. She was in an almighty yank to be off."

"It is very strange, but perhaps the visit was urgent—Lady Grieve dying, I mean. No doubt Linda left word for Richard to follow as soon as he awoke."

"You would think that would be important enough for her to wake him. You don't suppose the sly puss is up to something, Eve? She didn't even take a servant for company."

"What could she be up to? She made no secret of her going. If Ruthven feels Richard ought to know, he will tell him. I shall ask Ruthven to tell Richard we are off to London. Would you mind notifying the servants we are going, Hennie?"

"We will want to take Cook along, and Mary or

Sukey to make the beds and keep the saloon dusted."

"You are right. Tell them to get ready at once." I dashed off my note and sent Tumble over with it while Hennie arranged matters with the servants.

Hennie and I went upstairs at once to oversee our packing. As there was a possibility Richard would be in London, I meant to take a gown for evening wear. I did not forget, in all this confusion, that he still had my jewels. To ask for them back was as good as admitting I mistrusted him. That would be the end of my romance. I was not ready to sink it yet.

I expected every moment that he would come, but after half an hour, it was Ruthven who came. I went to speak to him. "I am upset at Lady Filmore's sudden departure, Ruthven," I said.

"I was upset myself at first," he replied, "but Mr. Dalton feels there is nothing amiss. Lady Grieve has been ailing for some time. Lady Filmore is her heir, you know."

That explained the mystery to my satisfaction. How eager Linda must have been to secure the fortune that would enable her to marry Harelson.

"Will Mr. Dalton be going to London?" I asked, trying not to reveal my eagerness. I was still eager, in spite of all.

"He asked me to give you this," Ruthven replied, and handed me a note. He remained there while I read it, in case an answer was required.

My darling:

Forgive my not coming in person. Ruthven has just roused me from a deep sleep. I am covered in whiskers and bruises after last night's escapade, and unfit for a lady's eyes until my valet pulls me into shape. I shall not detain your departure for London, as I know you are eager to leave. I want a word with Ketchen before going. I shall call on you this afternoon in London. Love, Richard.

P.S. A thousand apologies for last night's farouche display. And I forgive *you*, too.

I could not enjoy my billet-doux with Ruthven's knowing eyes on me. "No reply is necessary," I said, and he left, smiling to himself.

After he had gone, I read the note half a dozen times, reveling in its tone. "My darling." He had never used such terms of endearment before. He was coming to London. There was nothing amiss in Linda's precipitous flight. She would inherit her aunt's fortune and marry Harelson. In short, my headache was banished, the sun was shining, and I was ready to undertake my little jaunt with a light heart.

Chapter Twenty

AFTER RECEIVING RICHARD'S note, I was much inclined to delay my departure and go to London with him. By means of diligent dallying, I was still not ready to leave when Ketchen's rig pulled in next door thirty minutes later. Hennie sat with me in the saloon.

"There is Ketchen!" I exclaimed. "I wonder if he has any word on my silver. I believe I shall ask him." I jumped up instantly to run next door.

Ruthven had put Ketchen in a little parlor to wait. Rather than shunt me aside to this inferior room, he brought Ketchen to the saloon, saying that Mr. Dalton would be down shortly. I asked Ketchen if there was any news of my stolen belongings.

"I fear you cannot hope to hear of them for weeks, Miss Denver," he explained. "We'll not get a line on them until they show up at Stop Hole Abbey, or some secondhand dealer's shop. I have added your silver and picture to our list of stolen goods that we take around to the dealers. You might take a look at the description and see if it is accurate."

He handed me a distressingly long list of purloined goods. There at the bottom was a vague description of my silver and picture. "Place setting for twenty-four, sterling silver, rounded end with embossed design." It would describe half the silver in the country. I knew then that my silver was gone for good. I ran my eye up the list of other stolen goods. Lady Castlereagh's name caught my eye.

Right beneath it was a Mrs. Calhoun—of no interest herself, but she had been relieved of a "star sapphire ring, cabochon cut, edged in diamonds." I emitted a gasp of astonishment.

"What is it, Miss Denver?" Ketchen asked.

A dozen thoughts battled in my mind. There could not be two such oddities in England. I knew where that ring was; what kept my tongue between my teeth was uncertainty as to where Linda had got it. From Harelson, she had said, but she swore Hennie to silence, which suggested some double dealing. Her strange flight to London still bothered me. The awful notion arose that she was a part of Tom's ring herself. She often complained of a lack of money. But she was not clever enough to organize the thefts herself. Was she in league with Harelson?

Or had Harelson learned of her crimes, and was trying to sever any connection with her? It was not a long leap from Linda to the idea that her brother was involved. Why else had Richard blandly accepted her dart to London alone on the stage?

"What is it?" Ketchen repeated.

"Imagine the gall, robbing the foreign secretary's house," I said weakly. "I see the Castlereaghs were victims."

"Tom would rob the king himself without blinking."

I made a show of reading the list, to hide my confusion. I should tell Ketchen about that ring, but something held me back. Misplaced loyalty, perhaps. I had suspected Richard of duplicity regarding Lady Dormere's ring, too, but he had been telling the truth. I looked for the name Lady Dormere. After a careful scanning, I knew it was not on the list.

"Is this all of Tom's suspects?" I asked.

"All that we know of," he assured me.

"I see." I rose on trembling legs. "I am in a hurry,

Mr. Ketchen. I just wanted a word with you about my own lost items. I shan't wait to see Mr. Dalton. Good day."

I left and scuttled back home to think. I went into the garden; I sat on a bench, hidden by a wall of yews. It did not take me long to figure out that Richard had been making a game of me from day one. His object was to get my jewelry, and anything else that was not nailed down. He had either sneaked to London himself, or sent his minions to remove my Rembrandt. He was the only one who knew it to be a Rembrandt. I, like a fool, had played directly into his hands.

What bothered me much more was my jewelry, even now in his vault, unless he had already moved it. I must recover it at once, and what better time than while a Bow Street officer was in the house? I hated to do it, but I took myself by the scruff of the neck and headed back toward Dalton's. Ketchen was just coming out the door. I gave a shout and caught his eye. I led him into the garden, to avoid Hennie.

"Mr. Ketchen, you intimated last night that Mr. Dalton might be Tom, the burglar, if I am not mistaken?"

His ferretlike face grew sharper. "That I did. Right queer he is acting this morning, too. Sending for me, and when I call on him, he does not see me, but only asks for my list—that same list I showed you, Miss Denver. Very odd behavior."

"This may take a while. You had best remove your gig from in front of his house. I'll ask my gardener to run it around to the back. There is a road that leads behind the house."

I did this, then we resumed our conversation. I told him about the sapphire ring, and about Lady Filmore's sudden dart to London, and confessed that my jewelry was in Dalton's house.

"What excuse did Lady Filmore give for going?" he asked.

"Her aunt, Lady Grieve, was ill. Dalton backed her up."

"They lied to you; Lady Grieve went to her estate in Hampshire a week ago. She always notifies Bow Street to keep an eye on her house when she leaves town."

"Then where did Lady Filmore go?"

"She was not on this morning's coach, for I was passing by as it was loading. I would have noticed her. That pair are up to something. I am very happy you notified me, Miss Denver." He rose in some excitement.

"Are you going to get my jewelry?" I asked hopefully.

"You will get it back when Tom Cat is captured. He will be meeting up with his sister for some sly tricks. I shall have my rig ready to follow when he leaves."

"You'll never be able to keep up with him in your gig. Take my carriage," I offered. "It is not as fast as Dalton's, but I doubt he will attract attention to himself by driving sixteen miles an hour."

"That is what I call cooperation!" He beamed.

"There is one condition, however. I insist on going with you." I wanted to be there when Dalton was led away in manacles. That would teach him to call me his darling, and lie to me, and steal my goods.

"Now, there I fear I cannot oblige you, ma'am."

"Then you had best send off to the hiring stable, for I shall follow Dalton when he leaves."

"It could be dangerous."

"I hope you have your gun. Dalton carries one in his side pocket."

I rose and strode away. I found Luke weeding the garden, and sent him for my carriage, then I went into the house to tell Hennie of the change of plans.

Ketchen followed me, trying to convince me to give him my carriage for his sole use.

Hennie could not resist a little jibe. "Why, you never mean it was *your* beau all along who is the thief, and here you thought it was mine?"

"I do not rule out the possibility that Brockley is in on the plot," I told her, though I did not believe it.

"Do you want me to go with you?" she asked.

"Not *two* ladies, I beg of you," Ketchen said.

I took this for capitulation that he would tolerate one, and told Hennie she need not put herself to the bother.

Ketchen went to get his pistol from his gig while I put on my bonnet and pelisse. We waited by the window to see when Dalton left. It was not two minutes before he came darting out of the house as if the hounds of hell were after him. He drove his traveling carriage, harnessed up with a team of four. John Groom had managed to get it home safely, with no harm to the horses. I recalled Richard saying he drove his coach and four last night to convince anyone watching that we were driving to London. He was pulling the same stunt today.

We let him get a little distance down the road before following after him. He drove east, not north toward London. I recalled that Naismith had mentioned Eastbourne, and mentioned it to Ketchen. "Could that be their headquarters?"

"It could very well be. We have been thinking, at Bow Street, that Tom has some out-of-the-way place he hides his loot until it is safe to sell it. Dalton used his connection with Townshend to ferret out news. He would not sell any item that was on our list, for fear of being caught."

"How does it come that Lady Dormere's emerald ring, which she says was stolen by Tom, was not on the list?"

"If it was not on the list, then it was either not

stolen, or she did not report it. The latter seems unlikely."

"Yes, it does." I wondered how Dalton had got hold of her stationery to write me that note. Every word Ketchen uttered confirmed my suspicion that Dalton was the thief.

We had no difficulty following his carriage for the first few miles. There was just enough traffic that we could keep a few rigs between us, in case Richard was peering over his shoulder. On the far side of Rottingdean we hit a patch of road with no rigs, and he whipped his team up to a speed we could not match. His carriage began pulling farther and farther ahead, and finally disappeared around a bend in the road.

I feared we had lost him, for there was any number of side roads he could have taken. We assumed he was headed for Eastbourne, and bore on in that direction, eventually spotting him ahead of us again.

"I would give a goose to know what set him off," Ketchen said, peering narrow-eyed through my carriage window.

"Perhaps Lady Filmore told him Mrs. Henderson saw the sapphire ring. He might suspect I had seen your list of stolen items when you remained behind last night."

"I daresay that is it. It don't account for Lady Filmore's sudden flight, though, does it?"

"No, it doesn't."

"Perhaps the young lady is innocent," Ketchen suggested. "I mean to say, she let Mrs. Henderson see the ring."

"Yes, but accidentally. And that still does not explain her flight."

We continued toward Eastbourne. On a less nervous day, it would have been a pleasant drive. The ocean gleamed beside us, sparkling like a giant sequined gown in the sunlight. A fresh sea breeze blew through the carriage. It was getting on toward noon when we arrived at Eastbourne, a pleasant little seaside town, sheltered by the South Downs. Dalton slowly drove along the sea road that houses several inns. He made a brief stop at most of them.

I did not really want to see Richard captured. My heart was like lead throughout the entire morning. All my pleasant dreams were swept away, leaving before me the desolate knowledge of his treachery.

Several times Dalton stopped and looked all around. As he would recognize either Ketchen or myself, we set my groom the job of following him, and arranged to meet Topby in an hour at a tea shop. I cannot remember ever having spent such a futile, enervating morning. Topby returned a long hour later to inform us that Dalton had made a tour of all the inns on the beach strip, and there was a large number of them. Topby proved an ingenious accomplice. He had given one of the inn clerks a pourboire to discover what Dalton was up to. "He is making inquiries for a young lady, blond, attractive."

"Lady Filmore!" I exclaimed.

"Aye," Topby agreed. "And he is asking who she is with."

"Well now," Ketchen said, and fell into a frown. After a while he said, "Miss Denver, it is possible you have led me astray here. Lady Filmore could be in on this business without her brother's knowing it until she sheered off on him. As he is looking for her, they have not conspired to meet."

I snorted. "If there was any leading astray, Mr. Ketchen, pray remember who first suggested Dalton as the villain!"

It seemed that Dalton had visited every possible establishment in the town—shops, hotels, three vicarages, according to Topby—before stopping for a bite at a tavern nearby.

"He must suspect she is making a runaway match," I said.

"With young Harelson?" Ketchen asked sagely.

"Who else? She is engaged to him. We have come on a fool's errand, sir. If Richard is only trying to conceal Linda's romantic folly, I have no wish to interfere." Nor did I wish him to know I had come hounding after him, filling Ketchen's ears with my unfounded suspicions. "Let us go home."

Topby cleared his throat in a meaningful way. "Harelson, did you say, miss? Lord Harelson?"

"Yes, what other Harelson is there?"

"I saw him half an hour ago."

"What? Where?"

"On a side street. He was just going into a house. There was no sign of Lady Filmore. I would recognize the house."

"Good God! Why did you not tell me?"

"You never mentioned Lord Harelson. I thought it was the Daltons you were looking for."

"Take us to the house at once, lad, and be quick about it," Ketchen said, and we darted out to the carriage.

Chapter Twenty-one

"WAIT!" I SAID, and gave the check chord a yank. "We should tell Mr. Dalton. If he is only looking for his sister—well, it is fourpence to a groat she is with Harelson."

"I never could believe he was Tom," Ketchen had the gall to say, right to my face. I stared in dumb disbelief. " 'Twas yourself accused him. I only wondered if Townshend was wise to tell him so much of our business."

"Go and tell him what Topby said," I commanded stiffly.

"I am not your servant, miss!"

"Who do you think pays your salary? I am a taxpayer."

"Aye, you and every mort I try to help ends up throwing that in my face. What excuse can I give him for being here?"

"For God's sake, Ketchen, *go*, before he gets away."

"You'd best come with me, for to make some explanation."

I got out of the carriage and marched quickly down to the main street, just as Richard was giving his groom the office to leave. John Groom recognized me, and stopped. Richard looked out of the window to ask what was amiss, and spotted me. You would think he had seen a giraffe at least. He looked completely witless. "Eve, what are you doing here?"

I replied, "Are you looking for Harelson and Linda?"

He gave a shamefaced look and said, "Yes."

"My groom saw Harelson. We'll follow him."

I hopped into Richard's carriage and told Ketchen to tell Topby to lead the way. While we followed them, Richard said, "I fear the ninnyhammer has run off with Harelson. We had an argument last night. Linda told me a Cheltenham tale about his family cutting him off if he did not marry Agnes Carter. Agnes's engagement to some other fellow was in the papers a week ago. I told Linda so, but she would not believe me. She asked me to make her a generous marriage allowance. I refused. If Harelson cannot afford to keep a wife, he has no business getting married. I went to her room after Ruthven wakened me this morning, and saw she had hastily packed."

"What of Lady Grieve's illness?"

"I fobbed you off with that tale, to hide Linda's shame. I hoped to find her before they got the knot tied, and bring her home. I fear she and Harelson already have a special license."

"Why did you pick on Eastbourne?"

"Because Harelson comes here often. He has a friend who has a house in town, but I have not been able to discover it. Linda's note said she was going to London, so I knew that was the last place she would be." Next came the question I had been dreading. "How do you come to be here, Eve?"

"I fear I have bad news for you, Richard," I said, conning my mind for the least damning way to word my reason. "Linda accidentally showed Hennie a ring that Harelson gave her. I saw by Ketchen's list this morning that it is one Tom stole."

He looked positively blank. "You mean Harelson is mixed up with Tom?" he asked.

"It looks that way." I said not a word about either

Linda or himself being anything but a dupe. "He asked her not to show anyone the ring."

"When did he give it to her?"

"She has had it for months. How did he come to do such a foolish thing as to give her a stolen ring?"

"He was hot to marry her, when he thought she was wealthy in her own right. She was seeing another fellow at the time. I expect this was his way of securing her imaginary fortune. He thinks that by marrying her, he will force my hand to give her an allowance."

"And if he is Tom, or mixed up with Tom, he thinks you will not say so, when he is a part of your family."

As we spoke, the carriage rattled along, coursing up and down those pretty shaded streets of Eastbourne. Suddenly a "Hoi!" rang out, and the horses drew to a stop.

From his perch, Topby pointed to a brick house, smaller than a mansion, but it had a fine entrance with a pediment and fanlight. It looked like a respectable tradesman's residence.

Dalton squared his shoulders. "You had best stay in the rig, Eve." He removed the pistol from the side pocket, stuck it into the waist of his trousers, got out, and smoothed his jacket over it. Ketchen ran back to join us. They both insisted I remain in the carriage, so I did. It seemed wise to have someone outside to run for help, in case they did not come out.

They went to the door and knocked. No one replied, and after a moment's hesitation, they went in. The door appeared to be on the latch. I sat, watching and listening for perhaps ten minutes. I was on nettles, expecting to hear gunshots, or to see someone come hurtling out the door. When I could stand it no longer, I left the carriage and decided to sneak in by the back door. Imagine my astonishment to see, over the vine-covered fence, a wedding in progress.

Linda, as pretty as ever in a pale pink gown and the leghorn bonnet from her portrait, stood beside Harelson, who was rigged out in formal dress. A minister stood with the prayer book before his face. Another lady, a total stranger, completed the party. While Richard searched the empty house, Linda was being hitched for life to a man who was penniless at best, and at worst, was the infamous cat burglar. I opened the gate and rushed in, just as the minister said those fateful words, "Let him speak now, or forever hold his peace."

"Stop!" I shouted.

The little group turned and stared at me in alarm. The minister lowered his prayer book, and I found myself staring at the handsome blond man who had sold Lady Dormere's emerald ring to Parker in London. Clive Naismith, Grindley had called him. Robert, I thought to myself. A minister of the church stealing jewelry? A second thought told me it was more likely a thief was posing as a minister, performing a mock marriage. A "wife" would be easily led to conceal her husband's crimes.

They all stared in confusion. Linda said, "Eve!"; Harelson said, "Miss Denver"; the "minister" dropped his prayer book and said to Harelson, "Who the hell is that woman?"

I went pelting forward, confident that Richard and Ketchen would not be far behind. "You cannot marry Harelson, Linda," I said. "He is Tom, the burglar—or his friend is." I gave the "minister" a scathing look. "Did you get a fair price for Lady Dormere's emerald ring that you sold to Mr. Parker, sir?"

The man turned white and said, "She's fly to our rig, Harelson."

"Stubble it, Clive," Harelson said under his breath, but in the quiet afternoon, I heard him. So it *was* Clive. Grindley was not present, so I acquitted him of involvement.

Linda gave me a cross look. "How did you get here?" she asked. Then she turned back to Harelson. "You may be sure Richard is not far behind. Let us finish the ceremony at once."

"Are you not listening?" I shouted at her. "That sapphire ring Harelson has been trying to get back from you was stolen by Tom the burglar. You must not marry him."

Harelson and the "minister" exchanged a determined look. It was the latter who came pacing toward me. I noticed that Harelson had a crushing grip on Linda's arm. Before long, Clive had me in a similar hold. All trace of civility had left them. Linda was shrieking; I was kicking and shouting "Richard!" at the top of my lungs. Where was he?

"Shut your face," Clive said. I felt something hard prodding my back and assumed it was a pistol. I fell silent. While the men herded us toward the house, the female witness darted to look into the street. I was frightened, but real terror was held at bay by the knowledge that rescue was at hand.

The woman came pelting back. "There's two carriages out there," she told Clive. "Nobody's in them but the grooms. Best not take these hussies into the house. We might have company."

"I came alone," I said. "One of the carriages is mine."

"What about the other?" Harelson asked.

"It will be Richard's," Linda said, the ninnyhammer. She behaved in an absolutely incomprehensible manner. She did not appear to be frightened, yet she did not seem to consider it a game either. She looked confused and annoyed with us all.

Harelson darted toward the front of the house and was soon back. "It's Dalton's rig," he said to Clive. "We've got to get the ladies out of here. Marion, bring my carriage around to the rear of the house."

Marion ran off to do as she was bid. We were now two against two, but unfortunately two strong men against two unarmed women.

"We can't leave Dalton alone in the house," Clive objected. "He'll find the stash." Linda frowned dumbly.

"I'll take care of Dalton. You get the ladies out of here," Harelson said. As he was giving the orders, I figured he was the ringleader. Lord Harelson was the infamous burglar, and here I had thought him quite a swell.

I had not noticed when Harelson drew out his pistol, but he suddenly had one in his hand. He slid it into the waist of his trousers before going into the house. It was now two unarmed women against one armed man. The possibility that Richard and Ketchen would come to our rescue was lessened considerably. If Harelson managed to sneak up on them . . . He knew the layout of the house. I had a dreadful vision of Harelson shooting Richard in the back, and knew I must move speedily. I scanned my surroundings for a weapon. There was a stout branch on the ground behind Clive.

Clive made no effort to restrain our arms, but he moved the gun back and forth between us. Linda was fussing with her leghorn bonnet. "This is a fine way for a minister of the church to act," she said to Clive. "I shall report you to your bishop when I return home."

Clive just grinned at her simplicity, then winked a conspiratorial wink at me. I opened my reticule, planning to "accidentally" drop it and pick up the branch. The difficulty was that I would have to drop the reticule two feet from me.

"No tricks if you know what's good for you," Clive said, and dashed the reticule from my hands.

"You are very rude!" Linda said, stepping closer to him.

I bent down to rescue my reticule. I heard Clive

say, "You may see worse than this before the day's over, milady."

I made a lunge and picked up the branch. Linda saw what I was up to. I fully expected her to give the show away, but I think she was beginning to understand our situation. She smiled flirtatiously at Clive. "What do you plan to do to me?" she asked, in a coquettish voice.

I raised the branch and swung it at his head. He was thrown off balance, but not knocked unconscious. His head was obviously harder than wood.

"Hit him again!" Linda squealed. I swung at his stomach the second time, and he doubled over in pain.

Linda snatched his gun while I ripped off his cravat and bound his hands behind his back. This was accompanied by a string of proficient oaths and curses—from Clive, I mean.

Soon other curses rent the air. It was Topby, pelting toward us, gaping in wonder. "Lordy, Lordy! What is afoot, Miss Denver? I saw Harelson peering over the gate, and thought I should investigate."

"Harelson is in the house with Dalton and Ketchen. He has a gun. Secure this lout to a tree, and run for a constable as fast as you can."

"You're never going in there!"

Linda handed me the gun, smiling apologetically. She glanced at Clive. "He isn't a *real* minister, is he?" she said.

"If he's a minister, I'm a nun. Let us go." I snatched up my reticule, for I had brought a good deal of cash with me.

Topby took out a clasp knife and cut down a clothesline. He walked toward Clive in a determined way. Linda and I went cautiously into the house. The last thing I expected to hear was laughter, but Richard's unmistakable laugh rang out. It came from abovestairs. There was no sign of Harelson. We crept into the kitchen and followed the sound of laughter to the foot of the stairs. Harelson was just coming down, his hands bound behind him, while Ketchen and Richard followed.

"Eve! I told you to stay in the carriage," Richard said.

I looked at Linda, wondering what she would say to Harelson, and what he could possibly say to her. He looked thoroughly ashamed of himself. He hadn't the bottom to look at her, or to apologize. He just stared at his feet, while his face turned from white to scarlet.

She pulled the sapphire ring off and put it in his pocket. "I won't be needing this," she said. A tear glittered in her eyes. I never saw her looking lovelier than she looked that minute, with her pretty little face crumpled by sorrow.

"That there is evidence, milady," Ketchen said, and recovered the sapphire from Harelson's pocket.

We all stood at the foot of the stairs. Sunlight came in at the windows, painting rectangles of light on the parquet floor. Dust motes floated languidly in the rays of sunlight. For a moment, there was not a sound.

"The other man, Clive, let out the loot is in the house," I said to Richard.

"We found it. Ketchen will take it into custody." He turned to Linda, who was dabbing at her eyes with a handkerchief. The frustration was easy to see on his face, but there was sympathy there, too. "I'm sorry, sis," he said, and she fell, sobbing, on his chest.

It seemed best to get her away from Harelson, so I suggested she and Richard and I go into the saloon for a glass of wine, while awaiting the constable. I left them alone for their explanations while I ran upstairs to get a look at Tom's loot, before it was taken away. I found it in the master bedroom, in a wooden trunk on the floor. All manner of jewelry: diamonds, pearls, rubies, set in necklaces and bracelets and rings. A king's ransom in gems. There was no cash. That they used as quickly as it came in. I later learned the plan was to take the jewelry to the continent, and sell it there.

I found my silver and my Rembrandt in the clothespress. They were the only things other than cash and jewelry that Tom had taken.

That night, after we were all home and the criminals were incarcerated, Richard told me why. "It was a ruse to get you to London, so Tom could search Lady Grieve's house for your jewelry. He drove to London after Brockley's party, and was back by morning."

"Odd he did not search my house in Brighton after all."

"Not really. Last night, after having robbed your London house the night before, Mrs. Henderson saw Linda wearing the sapphire ring. He was afraid Linda would tell the whole, as she did. He knew that if it reached my ears, I would recognize it at once, and suspect he was Tom. He set up this runaway wedding, feeling I would be forced to hold my tongue when he was married to Linda."

"It cannot be a real wedding! Clive is not a minister?"

"He did take holy orders. Later he went to the bad."

"I wager Harelson knew it was Clive with Grindley last night, when he assured me it was Robert." Richard nodded.

"Clive was a school chum of Harelson's. Harelson was the brains of the gang. He mixed with society to ferret out vulnerable houses. He first did the stealing himself, then he got the idea that it would be safer to have a sterling alibi for some of the robberies. That is when he called in Clive. When they were short of blunt, Clive would risk pawning a few pieces in certain shops where no questions would be asked."

"Like Parker's place."

"Exactly. If I had seen Clive at Parker's that day, I might have figured this out sooner. He must have left just before I arrived. As soon as he got the money, he would hop back to Eastbourne. He did not mix in society at all. He and his wife pass for gentry. She was part and parcel of the outfit, but her husband did the gentlemanly thing and pretended she was innocent. She will not go to trial."

"How is Linda taking it?"

"As well as can be expected. I cannot be too hard on her. As he came from a good family, I did not check his bona fides as I should have. I feel sorry for his family. He was left a competence, but ran through it years ago. He has kept up appearances since then by thievery."

"Don't be too hard on yourself, Richard. I never suspected him either."

He turned to me and said, "You never did explain how it came you were at Eastbourne, Eve."

"Surely I told you this morning? Hennie told me about the sapphire ring; I took the idea it might be a runaway match."

"Linda had a note from Harelson asking her to meet him by the Steyne. But you did not follow Linda. You came over to my house some time after that." He looked a question at me.

"I have been wondering why you called Ketchen this morning, Richard. Had you seen Linda's ring, and wanted to verify that it was on his list of stolen items?"

"No, she never showed me the ring. If I had been closer to her, she would have confided in me."

"Don't blame yourself. She needed a firm hand."

"I suspected no more than a runaway match. I thought Ketchen might have heard rumors if Harelson was in debt. I asked him to bring the list as an excuse, but impatience—and discretion—got the better of me, and I decided to keep it to myself. Er—how did you say you came to be in Eastbourne?"

There was no getting out of it. "Ketchen told me Lady Grieve had gone home to Hampshire—in perfectly good health."

"So you suspected I was on the trail of a runaway match and followed me," he said, thinking he was pretty clever. "You were correct to think I would not have let you come with me."

"But I came in handy after all, did I not?"

"A lifesaver," he said warmly.

To divert him, I said, "I noticed Lady Dormere's emerald ring was not on the list of stolen items, Richard."

"It was on an earlier one. Bow Street removes items as they are recovered. They update the list on a weekly basis."

I nodded, as though it were only a minor detail.

With business out of the way, Richard lifted my fingers to his lips and said, "How shall I ever repay you?"

"By trusting me the next time," I replied with a moue.

"I feared you would think us a family of yahoos. I wanted to hide Linda's shame from you."

"She was a victim. One can only feel sorry for her."

"Your friendship will mean a good deal to her now, Eve. You are the only lady she can confide this secret in."

My breast swelled with pleasure. In future, I would be Lady Filmore's bosom bow, one of the charmed golden circle. "Please tell her I am always here, if she wants to talk to me."

"We mean to make very sure of that," he said softly. His eyes glowed as he drew me into his arms for a ruthless kiss. From the edge of the universe, I heard the door knocker sound. It might have been a million miles away. I ignored it and gave myself up to the luxury of loving and being loved. I did what I had wanted to do forever; I ran my fingers through his crisp black hair, tracing the contours of his well-shaped head, claiming it for my own while our lips clung.

Richard took similar freedoms with my anatomy. His hands moved possessively over my back. One inched forward, brushing my cheek, and inflaming me until I feared I would swoon. I had to turn my head aside, for I felt I was suffocating from love.

"We feel the best way of insuring your company is by making you one of the family," he murmured against my cheek. "Darling, will you marry me?"

"I shall give it serious consideration, Richard," I said. A lady must not capitulate too swiftly.

"Your jewelry is resting in my vault. You were too naive to ask for a receipt. If you ever want to see it again . . ."

"That is coercion!"

"All's fair in love and war," he said, kissing me again.

More interruptions came from the edge of the universe. There was a discreet noise at the door, followed by the door opening. Hennie peeked in, just as we flew guiltily apart. She was followed by a blushing Lord Brockley.

She came mincing forward, holding out her splayed fingers, on one of which rested a diamond of immense size. "You'll never guess what, Eve!" she gurgled.

"Me, too! Only Richard has not given me a ring yet."

We all congratulated one another and laughed and talked quite nonsensically for an hour. "A willing foe and sea room" was not the evening's toast, but Brockley did not completely leave off his naval talk.

"I hoisted my colors, fulling expecting a volley of

cannon, but she let me aboard." He smiled. "I mean to take my lady to London to meet the queen."

"What nonsense," she simpered, "doddering into vogue at our age."

It was after eleven when our fiancés left. Hennie and I sat on the sofa, smiling like a pair of imbeciles.

"Imagine, me being Lady Brockley. I should be ashamed of myself," Hennie said, smiling besottedly at her ring. She did not mention what David would think.

"Nonsense! You should be shouting from the housetops."

"That's just what I feel like doing. Odd Richard did not give you a ring, Eve."

"He will. He mentioned a family heirloom." I was feeling generous. "It will not be so large as yours, of course."

"Ah well, he is not a peer. Folks won't expect so much from *Mr.* Dalton as they would from *Lord* Brockley."

"You must learn to curb your gloating, Hennie. It ill becomes a countess."

"Me, a countess! I can hardly believe it."

A countess, married to a short, squat little man with a balding head, who lives in a house that resembles a bordello. You must forgive me if I felt I was making the better match. I would not change Richard for a prince. Mind you, that family heirloom might be exchanged for a new, larger diamond ring, if Hennie continues in this uppity way.

More Romance from Regency